LOVECRAFT'S IRAQ

David Rose

COPYRIGHT © DAVID ROSE, 2022
COPYRIGHT © SCREAMING BANSHEE PRESS, 2022

All rights reserved. No part of this publication may be reproduced, distributed, or transmitted in any form or by any means, including photocopying, recording, or other electronic or mechanical methods, without the prior written permission of the publisher, except in the case of brief quotations embodied in critical reviews and certain other non-commercial uses permitted by copyright law.

1.

05 1334C SEP 2005

Corporal Josh Silver is on his face. His M4 beneath him, he rolls onto one side to free the rifle from the rest of his gear. He crawls toward the body of his team leader.

He screams, "Ellers is hit!"

Grabbing hot Iraqi earth, he crawls low, onward, towards rounds from an AK-47 that's exploding; kicking up sand and soil and the dry grass at his mouth. He spits it all out.

"Ellers!"

Ellers, Silver's team leader, had survived deployment after deployment, Purple Heart after Purple Heart.

Now this.

A fucking waste.

His team leader lays in the high weeds of the ditch, the ditch they'd been patrolling alongside of. But his legs are splayed out in the open sand. He has stopped moving. The entire team took out the Iraqi who shot him. Fucker had been burrowed in the weeds like some sniper. American grenades and the unloading of M4 rifles saw to his massacre, but another Iraqi is down in the ditch and still shooting. Every time Silver gains an inch, he is put back, back down by the *zing*s and *vweeep*s barking up out of the ditch and its weeds.

Gunfights had been few, but when they came, somehow, they were always the same: the noise first, seeing the enemy second— sometimes not until the Zaidon's persistent Mujahideen had been blown open by the artillery gun-lines back at Camp Fallujah. Silver can't see where this bastard is shooting from, but he realizes if he summits the small lip Ellers lays on, chances are high he'll be nose to nose.

"Ellers!" he yells over the gun fire. "Talk to me!"

Silver plants his knees. Digging his helmet into the ground, he arches his back to give his hand room to open a pouch on the front of his rig. He pulls out his last grenade.

The AK-47 suddenly goes silent. A mag change! Even the enemy had to do them. Silver shoots up, balancing, working a finger through the grenade's pin—

—A roar sends him back onto his belly, automatic fire, so close its shooter's boot stomps down on his calf muscle.

"Got that motherfucker!" says a voice.

Silver rolls onto his back, his rifle dirtied up, his grenade still clutched in his hands. Corporal Alexis Mangler blocks out the September sun, his M249 machine gun still smoking.

"Oh, Jesus," the other members of Stygian 2-3 say.

Corporal Jonathan Nguyen and Lance Corporal Chase Hutchinson were both working their way to the ditch when the Mangler had taken out the last shithead. Hutch and Nguyen watch as Silver tries to hold together their team leader's skull. That copper smell is in the air. The stickiness of blood soaks the ground as lieutenant-summoned helicopters buzz in the distance. Under Ellers' helmet, where a chickenshit round had made its way under, chunks of brains still glob and glisten.

"Stygian Two this is Stygian Two-Three," Corporal Nguyen speaks into the handset of the green brick radio strapped to his back. "We need," he was going to say the platoon corpsmen. "We got...we got one KIA. Over."

Chatter erupts in Silver's headset. He ignores whatever orders come rushing in, wiping the blood off his hands and onto his desert-pattern camouflage trousers. Every heart pounds. Pre-deployment training had run them through scenarios of dead and wounded. Tons.

But this was a first.

The first real one.

Silver looks up at the rest of Stygian 2-3: his team. Their eyes are reflecting his own reluctant revelation. The truest battlefield oddity: when it comes—death—it's numbing how not a big deal it is, how not a big deal it *feels* once over, not having happened to you. He reckons they may all feel something later.

Not just their platoon; Stygian 2, but platoons Stygian 1 and 3. And not just Alpha Company—as per tradition, renamed overseas to its blackened moniker—but also Bravo Company's now Hammer 1, 2, and 3. Every single platoon in 5th Recon Battalion had broken down their six-man teams into teams of five, allowing for the men to operate out of Humvees with team integrity. Stygian 2's platoon commander's knock-and-talk ended the moment that enemy sniper had taken his shot. Now, Stygian 2-3 was down to four.

Silence gave way to: "BDA?"

Nguyen had said it.

"Right," Silver says, taking Mangler's hand, getting back onto his feet.

A Battle Damage Assessment soon revealed that the second enemy hadn't made it far from his accomplice, maybe the length of one of the bongo trucks wheeling around in this post-Fallujah farmland.

An intent voice reappears in Silver's headset. *"Stygian Two-Three this is Stygian Two-Actual. Sitrep? Over."*

The platoon had been patrolling with such dispersion only now are the other teams ending their frantic runs to meet Stygian 2-3 alongside the ditch. The lieutenant and platoon sergeant are still somewhere else.

Silver sees Nguyen is looking at him, waiting. "Stygian Two-Actual," Silver says into the mic of his MBITR. "This is Stygian

Two-Three. There was another tango in the defilade. All clear now… over." Silver looks at his MBITR; the small black radio they all have strapped to their chests for inner-platoon and inner-team comm. He makes a point to remember, he'll have to listen to it a lot more carefully from here on out.

Wading through fetid water was nothing new. Marines became Recon by way of one hardship after the next, patrolling through sleepless swamps being one. When he gets to the dead sniper, Silver takes the Dragunov out of his mangled hands. Semi-automatic, gas-operated; the scoped rifle had taken a beating.

"Silver," Nguyen calls over. Nguyen and Hutch are both bent over the one Mangler had aced. The one with the AK.

"Yeah?" Silver says, tossing the Dragunov up to Mangler. "What's up?"

"Take a look at this."

Though coming down off a surge of adrenaline, these trained observers can't help but notice Mangler's precision. With an area weapon he'd turned to gore the top half of the Iraqi's face. The team ogles for a minute while helicopters and the rest of Stygian 2 hover at various points above the watery ditch. Seeing enemy dead somehow makes one feel better. *You got one, but we got two.*

Hutch is well-known as the platoon's Born Again. But as they move and kneel by their dead team leader, Silver can't hear Hutch's prayer. Silver's mind is still in the ditch, on the weight of his gear and the blood in the sand. It's on the men who kneel beside him and the one dead who they praise. Silver rises, feeling his burden. He is the team leader now.

2.

09 2041C SEP 05

Sergeant Paul Miller lifts himself up from his hospital bed. His meds are wearing off again, taking his mind off the bleak, tiny room and back onto his excruciating pain—abruptly ending where a bullet from a machine gun had severed his spine.

"Sarah!" he'd done it again. Correcting himself, he calls out into the hall, "I mean, *Holden.*"

The past three days, Miller's voice hadn't been the moans that had crowned their trysts. For months they'd gotten away with it. Not even Ortiz had known. Now their affair was just one more thing that was over. Now, Miller's calls were reduced to noises so pitiful he could hardly believe his ears.

That she'd eventually confessed she was married had bothered him, sure. But he was, at the end of the day, or so he told himself, just a man. A man with needs and a man in a job where contemplating his and other men's mortality was a daily occurrence.

He had made a point early not to beat himself up about the infidelity. In places like war-torn Iraq, and in 2005, such things came with the standard bundle of forgive-me-laters.

The aluminum walls thrummed with the rumble of an approaching motor.

Miller knew HM3 Sarah Holden was not only an airhead, but an airhead who couldn't be trusted. Do that to your dude back home, what confidence can you really give someone? But now, in the lunatic cosmic scheme of things, she was now his nurse; responsible for his well-being, the meds he needed right away, and the humiliating rituals that were sure to be done at least once more before his flight out.

His ears hadn't deceived him. It was that god-damned up-armored again. "Holden," he sighs.

"I'll be right there, Paul—Sergeant Miller."

"Head's back," Miller says as the Humvee outside comes to a halt on the gravel.

He would have pretended he was asleep, but he knew this asshole would just rouse him.

"Hey, sir, the old up-armoreds purrin' like a kitten."

Captain Whitehead scowls and scratches his high-and-tight. "How you feeling?"

"I'll live."

"That you will."

Ordained in fresh desert digis under body armor without so much as a mustard stain, the captain held his helmet proudly at his side the way a posterchild for the war may. More comical yet, Miller's English teacher back in Des Moines would be so proud. Irony: it walked and breathed and barked orders in the manifestation of his company commander. Not only was *Head*, despite the Iraqi sun, paler than snow, the guy had a huge god-damned head. It must have been that big brain that encouraged him to snake the company's one up-armored Humvee while the actual ground-pounders were reduced to getting blown to pieces in green Jeeps.

"Holden, for real this time!"

"Get in here, Holden," Head says over his shoulder before squaring himself and stating, "Sergeant Miller."

"Sir?"

"You're out of here. First thing tomorrow morning."

"Roger that," Miller sighs.

"You'll be returning a hero, Marine." Head sounded like he was practicing a speech. "I'm putting you in for the Bronze Star."

Miller hoped by looking down at his own legs he'd clue Head in that medals meant about as much to him as a pair of new running shoes. And a medal for what? He'd done nothing heroic. Only with the obscurity capable of a career officer did Head mew on about how popping that red star cluster out from the rubble had saved "Countless Iraqi lives."

Head was still droning on about the Hearts and Minds campaign. His favorite slogan, pulled out and whipped with impunity whenever his men needed reminding of the importance of winning over local nationals. "The world needs to hear these truths."

Miller laughs, laughs like a condemned man may if having heard his guard fart while walking him straight to the electric chair. Truth. Truth was no one would ever believe what had happened out there. Those, those *things*. "Last Iraqi's heart I put in my scope, sir, didn't fare too well."

It may have taken the sum of Head's blood to spasm his temples and redden his face. "Well," Head says, looking away. "Returning to a hero's welcome none the less," before having to add, "even if you did expose your team."

It was Miller's turn to grow red. That SEAL, what was his name—Marcus Luttrell? He was likely destined for fame and fortune by merely being spotted too, by a goat-herder no less. Miller doubted a juicy, nationalistic book deal would be coming his way though. All he'd get were Head's bullshit medals and a lifetime of pity.

Never be able to walk again. Is that what he'd heard the doctor say? He refused to believe it.

On to the topic of books, Miller noted, Head was reaching down for the tattered hardback he was holding.

"Ever heard of him, sir?" Miller hated things being snatched from his hands, though it amused him to see a second-rate former jock peruse a ragged copy of weird fantasy.

Head squinted at the yellowed pages before finally issuing: "My little brother loves this nerd shit. Useless, if you ask me."

"I know, sir, right? About as useful as our holy Hearts and Minds cam—"

"My two favorite Marines," Holden enters with the long-awaited cocktail.

"My favorite Corpsman," Head says, flopping the book between Miller's feet.

Miller didn't know what irked him more—that this dick would toss his book where he couldn't reach it, or how Holden was basting Head in the same flirty gestures that had proven so effective on him.

"Alright, Miller, we're heading to chow." Head smiles at Holden. "I won't deprive you of your nurse for too long."

Holden hands him his dinner. The IV tubes taped to his hands tighten and slack as he knocks back the cup of pills. Her tits were incapable of being subdued, even under the motley egalitarianism of her scrubs. He hid behind his allotted water cup, refusing to let those creeping thoughts prevail.

"Enjoy the meatloaf," he says.

Out in the evening, he hears two Humvee doors open and shut. Miller puts his earphones in, drowning out the diesel engine as it prowls deeper into the Marine compound.

The lights were timed to dim at 2100. Alone, in the darkness, Miller goes over his options: Gun store or fight valiantly with the career planner to prove he's still viable enough to wheel into base admin and hammer out per diem chits for fourteen years.

He wasn't done. It's all about surmounting challenges. He'd been commended his entire life for an ability to face adversity, realistically, even coldly, whether it be high school chemistry or boot camp or becoming the honor grad at sniper school. There were also those wheelchair Olympics. Miller switches to his gym playlist. *Blues Jam* by Henry Rollins comes on.

He rips the earphones out. He wasn't going to do shit—especially front squats anytime soon. He wouldn't be doing anything except flying to Germany then to Texas to take up a long career in therapy and collecting checks from the VA.

Wheelchair Olympian or not, no mollycoddled glory would ever compete with rising before dawn to dig into a three-day hide. To watch other grunts march bravely to pending doom, squeezing a well-known trigger, at just the right time, saving his brothers' lives while partaking in the ancient practice of spilling enemy blood.

He is a Scout Sniper, one of the deadliest men on earth. He'd shaken hands and clanked warm beers with heroes, the few warriors left in an age of why-me. His lower half had helped him carry rucksacks, sandbags, men smitten merrily by drink or dead by a gunshot wound to the head. It all felt so real. Too real for the pills steadily taking hold to lull him into believing he'd ever feel such things again. He cries out and punches the wall.

No longer operational, all that was left to do was wait and see how the after-action report would be cobbled together. "Nothing'll happen to that CAAT team," Miller says to thin air. Nothing. Some fuckhead LT will bury it—*it* being the lieutenant never told his platoon sergeant to spin their guys up on positive identification before laying a place to waste. No, the LT'll be free to pop his zits in peace and the platoon sergeant free to retire and be whisked away by the reemployment halls of Home Depot.

But those guys, that CAAT team, they were just baby-faced boots. Hell, he'd been one too his first pump to the sandbox. Maybe the idea that was sure to rise from a whisper up in Quantico and the Stone Bay schoolhouse would be the rightest. The blue on blue had only gone down because an entire Combined Anti-Armor Team had mistaken him for rifle-bearing Mujahideen, one who'd ran frantically past a farmhouse window. He'd compromised them. It was his own damn fault.

Miller's desert trousers were long gone. Apparently the sight of blood-soaked clothing, to speak of only one fluid, lounging on a chair next to their owner was bad for morale. His blouse, however, they'd let remain. With great struggle, Miller reaches over and pulls two sheets of paper from his left breast pocket.

The blood on one only further obscured a few words written in Arabic. No big loss. He was about as well-versed in that language as whatever the weird hieroglyphics were on the other page.

He puts them away. What those two pages had caused, what they'd allowed him to do, the images flashed in his mind...*horrid.* Horrid as the thought of having instead been paralyzed at the neck.

Or maybe they weren't *that* horrid. What happened was over. Never walking again, never playing soccer with the son he'd never have, these horrors were now just beginning. He couldn't hold his head up any longer. He feels the dampness of his pillow, then his eyes shut.

###

Three days prior, Miller had walked into the designated "take-a-shit" room of the house they'd confiscated. He pulled out his wag bag and assumed the position.

Ortiz had mentioned he'd seen a bunch of books stacked in the corner. Now level with the vellum and leather-bounds, his eyes caught an oddity; out of place like a hamburger or something, plopped in the midst of a Chinese buffet. Wedged between Qurans was the souvenir he'd end up keeping once hospitalized; an old short-story collection by H.P. Lovecraft.

Finished stinking up the place, he grabbed the book. Thumbing its worn edges, he tried to concoct how on Earth it ended up here. Had a vehicle patrol recently been by? Did some dipshit have an unsecured ruck bouncing on the outer shell of an open-back, or did haj here have a relative working as a janitor back at the compound who'd snaked it from a USO pile?

Miller flipped through the pages as he walked down a short hall to rejoin Ortiz behind their M40. This rifle had turned one guy to pink mist the week prior, and they, as the rest of their ilk, yearned for another.

Yet combat zones, if they could be anything, were often boring as hell. His few cohorts who actually read, all they swapped were harrowing accounts of Vietnam and *Black Hawk Down*. Going cover to cover with this horror stuff would be a welcome change.

When he bent down to recover two pages that had fallen to the floor, he saw they hadn't loosened themselves from the book. They'd fallen out of the book, but they were something else entirely.

One, its brown marring and brittleness suggested something incredibly old.

Though he'd never read anything by Lovecraft, Miller had played enough D&D growing up to have rolled funky dice and spilt soda cans with every stripe of nerdery. He'd heard about Cthulhu, stuff about penguins and racial blah blah, tentacles, and he'd heard of the Necronomicon.

Holding this ancient paper, trying to decipher its strange symbols mixed with all the Arabic, he couldn't help but laugh. That Arab guy, he recalled, the Mad something or other, he'd helped make the Necronomicon. Now here was Miller, smack dab in the Arab world, in possession of what looked to be one of the devilish tome's lost pages.

The second page, though creased and yellowed by time, was far newer. On this appeared to be sounded out translations, in English, of what was written on the first: *Morr, Gew, Raht.* A litany more.

Ortiz tapped his watch.

"Wait one," Miller mouthed, earning a furrowed brow from his spotter.

The homeowner was more or less how they'd left him. Hogtied and gagged with rigger's tape, the farmer lifted his head to see which American had entered then rested it back down on a water bottle.

As he peeled back the tape and cut the zip ties the old man's dry "shukran" made Miller have to look away. It was standard operating procedure; subduing and imprisoning whomever lived where they decided to set up urban hides or rural, trigger-worthy observation posts. Usually, it was an entire family. "Hearts and minds, my ass," Miller said as he helped the man to his feet.

There was a little time he could kill. Miller wanted to know. Though any traces of his granddad's worldliness had been obliterated, when prompted, the Iraqi spoke English okay enough. Aided by hand gestures and grim tones, the Iraqi explained his grandfather had been a Sunni religious cruiserweight, an eccentric who'd made the trip to Mecca and studied English along with other secular matters at the now bombed-to-shit University of Baghdad.

Apparently, his granddad, the Iraqi brooded, along with his uncles and even his own father had mysteriously vanished during one of their secret, all-male meetings.

The farmer eventually chalked it up to a bizarre yet heavenly reward; inheriting the house and the small plot of land it sat on. Not only that, but Allah had left him, wouldn't you know it, where all the men in his family had last been seen: a disheveled room full of books. Of no use to a farmer, they were stacked to gather dust.

The Iraqi knew the drill. He got on his stomach again as the Marine took a knee beside him. Miller was sure to set the zip ties to a bearable cinch. He bottle-fed the old man and was gleamed by a watery, snaggletooth grin when he decided to do without the gag.

Then Miller remembered. "Why did he translate?" Miller unfolded the newer of the two pages, holding it out. "Why did he write these sounds with English letters?" That Granddad had been a careful man, made sense further when the farmer explained everyone else in the family only read Arabic. "He didn't want any of you to read what he'd translated?" The Iraqi nodded. "Off this older page?" The Iraqi kept nodding diligently as most men would if prompted by their armed captor.

Miller knew guys who did a lot worse in these houses than take a damn book. He winked and waved it. Spoils of war. Besides, their sniper team always gave the homeowner a fat wad of Head-sanctioned dinar at the end.

Miller looked at the translations again. He sounded out the words in his head then placed the loose papers back in the book, stuffing it all down his cargo pocket. As he reentered the hall he uttered the words, absentmindedly, but aloud. In an instant the war in Iraq changed.

At first all he got was a strange look from Ortiz. Noise discipline was something they always followed with an almost religious fervor. But when the Iraqi erupted behind him, Miller felt the man's screams not only ring in his ears but crawl up his back and seize him by his heart. He swung around.

Though broad daylight, night had somehow swallowed the room. From the room's shade, darker shadows amassed into things, unable to be discerned as man or as beast. Then they swarmed the flailing, frantic Iraqi.

Gnashing doom wasn't leaving a thing, not even the entrails Miller saw spill or the blood that sprayed the walls hot red. Miller realized he was now on the floor. Ortiz had trucked him over and flown into the room.

Ortiz's M4 ignited the far wall in blinks of fire. Miller scrambled on his hands and knees out into the hall. Back at the M40, the rifle's green and bronze entered his hands with new, incalculable necessity.

Ortiz's gunfire stopped, resuming more frantically. During the mag change, Miller had heard Ortiz's succession of "Fucks!" derail into hysteria.

Night entered the hall, and along with it, Ortiz, landing as if having been thrown. On him bit and howled their enemy, shapeless, black, demonic—which had grown into no man.

Miller shouldered his rifle. The contents of an entire damn bolt-action were unloaded into one, but there were more.

Ortiz's large frame proved more difficult than the helpless Iraqi's. Ortiz fought them, kicking, clawing, then crawling down the hall towards Miller. Miller remembered, the claymore.

Placed at the rear door, meant to bat back ambushes or for an emergency egress, the anti-personnel mine would have to be angled high, high enough to just miss Ortiz, then be clacked to life.

Still holding his rifle, Miller ran. When he passed a certain window the house and his whole world was pummeled in a cataclysmic instant of pain and roaring noise.

The clock on the wall reads 03:34 when Head and Holden come in. *Chow?* Yeah right. Midrats had long been over. It was too easy to pretend he was still asleep. Grogged by the pills, Miller is waist-deep where he'd left off.

All those 7.62 rounds and that MK-19 must've killed those things as they were, Miller gulps down a reality too hideous to speak, as they were trying to *eat* Ortiz. He'd thought to ask Holden to ask around, but no reports of strange corpses or black, tarry blood was all the report he needed. They were gone. Only Ortiz's mangled meat had been scraped off the bricks and loaded into the back of a 5-ton truck.

Save for a few zonked-out patients also awaiting their ride on a plane, the hospital is empty. Now it includes, once more, his company commander and his dutiful nurse. It appears they'd been arguing; something they are determined to continue at the foot of his bed.

Head is pelting her with whispers. "Fine. You have the feels for him, okay. I'll write it up so it's the other guy's fault. That work for you?"

Holden looks like she's been crying. She mumbles something.

"Sure, Sarah," Head despairs, giving Miller a sideways glance. "Help me make this happen. I'll put Miller here in for the goddamn

Silver Star. I'll write him up a citation that'll make him a fucking hero, but I need this to happen. He'll never go along with how this has to play out. You know it. I know it."

"I can't!" Sarah shrieks, retreating to a corner.

Head's eyes grow wide. When he is sure Holden's outburst hasn't awoken Miller, he ceases his study of Miller's face to march over to her and tap the rank on his collar. "And I'll say it one more time, how 'bout I just send an anonymous email to that hick ass husband of yours? Show him all the fun you've been having? I'm not as fucking stupid as you. I can crop my head out."

Holden lurches forward and sobs into her hands. Miller feels like a spy in a movie. He'd remained still, though his heart is now racing. "Let's get this over with," Holden says suddenly, removing her hands from her face. "I won't say anything."

"Of course you won't," Head snarls. "Or you'll be rotting in the brig too. Now go get the morphine."

Miller watches as Holden opens a cabinet and pulls out every medical bag. The movie had ended. Miller put the pieces together as the two armed themselves with an arsenal of morphine injectors.

Head was going to doctor the official report, so his men had fought countless enemy. They'd saved lives of non-combatants, and, apparently to sate Holden's pang of guilt, Ortiz was now the man who'd exposed their team before their flawless victory had gone so awry. To tie up loose ends, and help seal his meteoric rise, Head was going to make it look like Miller had somehow gotten into the meds then proceeded to kill himself by jamming needle after needle into his tired, useless body. That he couldn't walk would be no match for a captain's pen.

One more suicide. One more PTSD hero.

Generals don't exactly approve of their men killing one another, accidental or otherwise. Blue on blue, when a combatant is killed by one of their own, just wasn't good for promotion.

They hold injectors like daggers.

And they advance.

Miller erupts from the bed. A punch to a man's groin never fails. Holden jumps back as Miller sends Head to the floor. *"Help!"* Miller cries.

No matter what he shouted, none would hear. Cries were something that went on all night in places where men waited to die. From under his blanket, he pulls out the papers. Beyond knowing, without thought, he begins to speak their words. Head rises with his teeth clenched, plunging a needle deep in Miller's thigh. Miller keeps reading. He feels nothing bad, then feels everything good.

So good he didn't care at all when Sarah stowed her tears to join Captain Whitehead in turning his legs into pin cushions. So good he didn't care when those ghastly things whirled into the room and devoured his killers.

Now it is quiet again and he is free to fade. Necronomic demons hover, the same ones he'd summoned to a swirling horde. Maybe it was *their* occupational specialty, he slobbered an untethered giggle, having recognized their time-void eyes, their listless sneer.

Miller knows the papers that he clutches, what it will mean when they are rediscovered. Their incantations uttered once more. He also knows protecting one's brothers must take on a whole new meaning.

Miller eats the pages so that nothing remains, then those who loom above his bed treat him the same.

When Miller comes to, his head swims with his intended killer; all that morphine. "Still," he mutters at the clock on the wall, staring at the red, unblinking 03:48. Head and Holden are gone. In one hand he holds the piece of paper he'd been too slow to swallow.

He holds it up and he squints. Licking his dry lips, the taste confirms he'd at least ate the old one. What he clutches now is what remains of the newer page, the one containing the sounds and magic that had been converted to English. Though he'd tried his best, tried with all his fury when he swore he'd seen his end not just coming but come, his best bite had only rid the world of the very line that had brought forth the demons.

There will be no more of those, those who must've devoured that Mad Arab Abdul Alhazred. He pukes.

They must've liked me, he thinks.

He looks down his body, across the vomit glistening off his gown, down his legs, what's left of them, at the injectors wobbling as he moves. He tries to sit up but the effects of those little would-be-deaths pin him to the bed.

No more walking. No soccer. No—*fuck all that!* He places the paper, the one with all the magic garbage, firmly in his mouth. He grinds his teeth and he grabs the siderails and fights nausea and delirium and the low throes of death to sit up and switch on the overhead lamp.

"Hey...hey you," he says, slobbers right after he takes the page out from between his lips, reminding himself of that song by Pink Floyd. Miller says it again, and again, to the corner housing the locker that had once housed med packs full of needles. "Tried to kill me, those two. Spared by goddamn ghosts." He chuckles, "But *they* weren't." He goes on like this until the clock turns 03:53, his mind getting no better.

It may have been his awakened heartrate, it may have been a lone injector; stuck in a fatty patch of skin, but steadily Miller worsens.

He jams a finger in his mouth. Again—this time to the knuckle where it stays until he's dry heaving and salty tears creep down his face. Injectors go flying to the four corners, some cartwheeling out into the dark hall as he fights the strange euphoria of slowed, slowing, shallowed-out lungs.

He inspects closer the line at the top of the page, the line just below where his bite had taken a chunk away. His lips move.

No sooner has he spoken than green flame leaps out to dance on the page's uppermost edge. What Miller finds strange, stranger than the fire, is the rough intuition telling him not to put it out. The flame persists, as ordinary fire does, save for the fact not a piece of the page burns away. One line of gibberish out of what had to be dozens had given him this.

He reads another. Then another. His heart almost beats to fear when the flame goes out and a low drawer in the med cabinet flies open. Tentacles burst, wiggling, grabbing at the air before slithering back. Next, a display of strange planets; brief and blue, swirls in the center of the room. The dance of these bodies shines and twirls and then they all fade, disappearing with an audible *pop*.

He scrutinizes the page now, each and every letter. Most of the phrases are strung together like the places in dictionaries where words are sounded out. Some are accompanied by drawings. One catches his eye: the unmistakable image of a flying bird.

This string of words is one of the longer lines, stretching from one side of the page clear across to the other. Scribbles and marks of an ancient erasure complicate his task. After baring down on the incantation long enough, hard enough, wrenching out one syllable at a time, he is finding that he is able to *feel*.

The bed thrums, then it stops. Something like lightning shoots through him, ending its electricity at his fingertips. He keeps reading. He keeps sounding out the litany, shunting all illness until all there is are his eyes and the words.

Sometimes, when dozing off in a hide, when his mind was no longer lethally alert, he would overlay what he was watching with memories of childhood. Quiet Iraqi towns reclaimed their life by the casual stroll of an ice cream truck, the skipping of children chasing its bells and clown-car noises.

Ever since he'd found himself crippled, he'd made a point not to drum up such visions. He has to admit that he is pleased to see the truck and kids again. But he isn't watching the scene unfold in farmlands, or on the page he holds, nor was the stock of his memory hallucinating itself into being on the sterile floor. They are entirely in his mind, kicking into action as he sounds out the final parts. Realer now than ever, he watches. The boys claw and bite each other. The girls smile; their dresses torn, their once-pink flesh mottled by decay. The ice cream truck is now on fire. His point of view changes. Black smoke rises to greet him, where he floats now, high above.

He stops reading. He is prepared to believe the morphine is killing him, sending him to Hell with a quick raping of what lingered of his innocence. But his lungs are not just recovering, they are billowing. He realizes now he is floating above his hospital bed, levitating level with the 03:58 of his room's dutiful clock.

Sweating, he leans to his left, rolling like a log, capsizing his world and sending him puking once more. Finally, he steadies himself. He feels the AC kick on, blowing cool across his face. He senses his soiled gown is swaying in the breeze, but he still cannot feel anything below where his spine had been severed. He concentrates on the space in front of him, just out of arm's reach. Slowly, but as certain now as the tentacles that had burst out from the drawer, he inches—he flies—across the open air.

Miller looks hungrily at the doorway.

Some heard laughter when he flew out of the hospital, beyond the compound, out into the wastelands. Out in the desert night, he finds a barren patch of earth. He conjures once more the green flames, giving him light as he speaks new and forbidden wonders.

Forbidden they are, but what man, even if aware the cosmic malignity he toyed with, so stricken by drug and torment, could truly care?

Sometime before daybreak, before the search for one sailor and two Marines would begin, before he devoured what was left of the final page, what was left of Sergeant Miller was replaced by the shrill cacophony of the insane.

3.

10 1507C SEP 05

"Yeah," Silver says, answering Greene's odd question. "Taps played all the way through."

Combat-zone funerals had become a highlight for the national news outlets. A pair of boots, sandbags holding tall a clean, upside-down rifle while dog tags hang from an empty magazine well. Then there was a flag, a folded or an unfurled one; lifeless or blowing in a desert breeze. The cameras sometimes showed all the particle board, the architecture that had become tables and walls or a speaking chaplain's pulpit. The outlets never showed when they went wrong, like a funeral Sergeant Raymon Greene had attended while in Afghanistan when the speakers fizzled during a fallen soldier's final song.

Sergeant Greene isn't Recon. The self-described "Brotha from St. Louis" is wrapping up his fifth year as a crypto-linguist. One of the few men in Camp Fallujah responsible for identifying foreign communications, to Silver, he is a walking brood of contradiction. Black, though he disliked all forms of rap. Fluent in Arabic, though he committed apostasy when he informed his Nation of Islam father, he believed in that shit about as much as a train ticket to Middle Earth. A great Marine, though his workspace was cluttered as, Silver assumed anyways, a frat boy's dorm room.

That Greene's unit gave him so much autonomy amused Silver. Especially, when contrasted against Recon's claustrophobic team rooms on the other side of camp, where a brother could be identified by laugh or break of wind. Sergeant Greene works alone, surrounded by a heap of signal equipment, radios, antennae, and flat-screen TVs; varying in their electric display from confiscated documents to unfinished games of solitaire. Greene's "office" being inside a Quadcon made no difference. From the outside, the 5' x 8' x 8' puke green box sat as glum as the rest. But inside, Greene had used foot lockers and caches of junk food to turn the place into a veritable nerd cave.

Greene sits in his office chair on one side of a particle board desk. Above him is a fluorescent light and bolted-in, portable ceiling fans. In front of him are ports for handheld radios and a desktop with cooling fans that never quiet.

Silver slides up a footlocker and sits across from Greene. He nods at a blown-up pdf on one of the screens. "What's that?" he asks, also noticing behind the screen lurks a Listerine bottle full of liquor.

Greene adjusts his glasses. "Something I drew." On the page is something that strikes Silver as a hieroglyph. Greene had drawn a large, upside-down T, crowned at its top by a hollow circle. On each side are markings. On one is something serpentine, slithering upward from the base. On the other are markings that make the whole thing look like a winged man, facing sideways, holding a curved sword.

"A day or two ago the Muj started talking about it," Greene says. "Talked about in not a good way, too. Something about seeing this tattoo on *new fighters*. They haven't shut up about it."

"Are you going to send this up the chain?"

"Nah, man—oh, and help yo'self," Greene says, watching as Silver reaches over and pours a shot.

"That's some weird shit."

"No," Greene laughs, pushing his chair away, wheeling over to a footlocker. A mess of soda cans and girly magazines spills out. Greene pulls from the heap a stack of books. "You wanna see weird?"

Silver is holding the Listerine bottle's top, full to the brim with what smells like Jack Daniels.

"Just a sec," Greene says, flipping through the pages, tossing one book, opening another. "Ah—here. Check it."

It was no secret why Greene loved hanging out with Silver. Silver was a genuine Recondo, a modern-day gunslinger. The reclusive, bespectacled crypto-linguist seemed nothing short of energized when asking him every question under the sun; from tactics, to ruck runs, to what it felt like to gear up and kick in doors. Silver loved hanging out with Greene because, with Greene, the atmosphere was always cool. Hidden in the confines of a humming Quadcon, it was the time where he could talk about whatever, whenever, without any worry over how the eat-our-own tribe of Recon may perceive him. They talked women, rock and roll, out-of-date movies, and—just as valuable—Greene was always full of surprises.

Nerd cave it was, for Greene holds open another book on Lovecraft. He taps on a page full of ornate symbols. "You see it?"

Silver doesn't answer, they were all just a bunch of—

"Now I do," Silver says. One of the symbols, about halfway down the page, looks almost exactly like what Greene had drawn. "So, what? You copied that drawing out of your book?"

"No, that's the weird thing. I mean, maybe it's some subconscious thing—like I've seen it and it messed with how I drew what I was hearing. But man, I don't think that's the case."

"You need to get out of this Quadcon more, Greene."

Greene shuts the book. He can't help but laugh. "Unless we got Muj out there playin' Call of Cthulhu board games, it's one helluva coincidence."

"What are all those symbols?"

"Elder Gods, Great Old Ones an' shit."

"Which one is that drawing about?"

"Not sure yet," Greene says, snatching the bottle top from Silver. "But I'm gonna find out."

Before Silver can transform his confusion into a question, the door swings open. Silhouetted by the sun, Nguyen is in full gear.

"Newjin," Greene smirks. "Need help with your radio?"

Nguyen looks at a pack of Newports on Greene's desk. "Those are going to kill you. LT's looking for us, Silver. We're going back out tonight."

4.

10 1601C SEP 05

"You're going on an OP," Lieutenant Ashton says to Silver. "You guys will be leaving the wire at midnight." Observation Posts are something Stygian 2's platoon commander loved more than haircuts. Stygian 2-1 had spent an entire week on one. Stygian 2-2 had stared at camel shit for four days back in the heat of August. Now it was the remains of 2-3's turn.

The platoon office is deep in Camp Fallujah, or the "MEK"; called such for reasons unknown to all. The room is in one of the low brick buildings that had existed long before the U.S. took over. The room is almost entirely white, lit damn-near to sterile by the fluorescents and no shortage of dry erase boards.

The lieutenant takes inventory of the team. Each well under the age of twenty-five. Each seated with their M4, clean, ready to go. Every man in the room sports a drop holster, hugging tight against their hip a M9 Beretta. Pistols mean little out here, but a secondary weapon is a sure sense of comfort, knowing rifles and machine guns can, and do, go down.

The team is looking back at their platoon commander, every one of them Recon and E-4s, except E-3 Lance Corporal Hutchinson. Hutch is still a 0311, the numeric code for the world-famous Marine Corps grunt. An infantry marine who'd come over to battalion but failed some vetting at the Basic Reconnaissance Course, due to the needs of the Corps, to say nothing of a recon unit stretched thin over the vast battlespace of the Al Anbar Province, Hutch had been allowed to deploy, integrated into a team and now operating as good as the rest.

It was impossible for Lieutenant Ashton not to smile approvingly at Nguyen, and *the Mangler*. Nguyen—now this was careerist potential. One of the battalion's most adept radio operators, this second generation American embodied not only patriotic zeal but the core values of Recon. The calm, silent professional's juxtaposition, however, scowled in the form of Alex Mangler. A barracks brawler and former golden glove, the Mangler was here for kicks. Those who doubted the ogre's intent all became believers when he insisted he patrol with the Para SAW. Though a M249 machine gun was designated for a team's junior-most, Hutch, according to Mangler, "Wasn't gonna be the one they called when they needed to bring the pain."

And then there is Silver. Not exactly absorbing the role of team leader, but Ashton affirms he holds promise. Right after Ellers' funeral, Lieutenant Ashton had informed Corporal Silver he'd been put in for combat-meritorious sergeant, and he'd be pinning him the first of October.

Lieutenant Ashton points to a dot on the map behind him and says, "Here's your home for the next two nights, gents. We got a farmhouse in our AO. Need some eyes on. I'm sure you've all heard by now we got three missing, a nurse over at Charlie Surgical and two Marines. I know fuck all how this all ties together, but everyone from general staff to the battalion commander is flipping out. More, we're getting reports from local intel that there are lights..." The platoon commander stops and walks over to his desk to check a paper. Returning to the large map on the wall. "...Green lights, and some strange noises too. All coming from said farmhouse. Apparently it got obliterated by a CAAT Team, but something may still be up."

"Sir," Hutch says. "Sounds like Terry Taliban's hostin' a rave."

"Taliban's not in Iraq," Nguyen says. "Hick."

###

The MEK's main gate is something right out of Mordor. Not by day, when the monotony of grey and brown stand eternal. But come nightfall, when the air cooled and the wild dogs begin to howl, the connecting T-barriers gave to those inclined a sensation of being in another world. This wall, some twenty feet high, bulked against the night. Because of its concrete, Silver can no longer see the moon from the back of their 5-ton as the multi-truck convoy rolls past, past the wall and Hescos and the foremost guard tower, out onto the warm asphalt of the MSR.

Main Supply Route Mobile and MSR Michigan; two of the main arteries connecting Fallujah to Baghdad and points east. The convoy isn't planning on spending much time on these. There are better, less traveled roads. Power line towers come and are then behind them. The trucks drive onto a confused junction, turning right, following a brief S curve, then they turn left, onto the next road.

The team can't see any of this. They can only feel the sways and bumps when their driver negotiates god-knows-what. Silver holds his map. The AL FALLUJAH 2-NIMA's laminated white bounces back the blue of his headlamp. So far, the convoy is making all the correct turns. He puts the map and headlamp back in his ruck and takes a breath.

Before their battalion landed, the already legendary Operation Phantom Fury had turned the city of Fallujah into hell itself. At great cost, anti-coalition forces had been decimated, or swept up into Abu Ghraib's notorious prison. But plenty enemy remained, die hard and infesting the southern farmlands this grim parade of Humvees and 5-tons are entering.

"Ready for this, *TL?*" Mangler elbows Silver.

Silver is rummaging. Triple-checking mission essential gear is good practice. All is there; the field sketch kits and the camera nobody knows how to use. "Yeah," he says, letting his hands rest. "Let's just hope Motor-T drops us off at the right damn place."

Mangler's SAW is resting on his lap. The machine gun's snub-nose points away from everyone, out into the dusty blackness.

No doubt warriors have looked upon their weapons in times of dread, when the enemy is too great, their end too near. Only the excitement that, too, comes with war could purse the lips of Hutchinson; gloss the motionless eyes of Nguyen as he holds his M4 up and wipes away sand from the grenade launcher just below its barrel. Silver checks his own. A 203 grenade launcher is cumbersome. Makes you rework your grip, but it's sure as shit battle-tested. The Mario Brothers grenades that *thwooped* out from the business end, if trained, could fly right through an open window.

An OP was lame. But Recon was more than fighting. An opportunity to conduct the type of mission that made their forefathers famous; this was duty, no matter how mundane, one to be accepted and carried out with minimal bitching.

The hardball soon diminishes to dirt.

Hitching a ride with a resupply convoy meant once 2-3 dismounts they will be virtually on their own. Sure, Nguyen's radio was one handset away from artillery—but Arty is no good if the Muj are overrunning you. The op order stated several infantry units were in the area, exactly who the trucks were bringing supplies to. But a bunch of trigger-happy grunts, misidentifying a recon team, could be just as dangerous as any terrorist.

Every axle feels the next one, sending a deep groan up into the canopy. Their benches squeak as the convoy makes a hard right.

"What do you think the green lights are?" Nguyen asks Silver over the clatter of the truck.

"If they exist," Hutch adds, then looks at Nguyen. "You see all the funky shit these people have in their shitholes? Could be a strobe someone keeps messin' with. Or maybe a—"

"Christ," Silver grabs some bench. "If *that* wasn't a pothole it was a goddamn mortar impact—and I don't know, man. I was thinking maybe we got a bomb maker."

"And the green?" Mangler asks.

Silver scratches his chin. "Welding?"

Hutch looks at his team leader. "Ain't gonna be nothin'. All this is comin' from *local intel*," he adjusts his dip with his tongue. "You know what *that* means. Buncha shady-ass Iraqis, tryin' to sell us somethin' they think we'd pay 'em for."

The rock and wave of the 5-ton carries them until Silver feels them slow to a crawl then start the hard left. "We're at the canal," he says.

Mangler whispers, "The one we were at the other day?"

"No, man." Silver snorts. "That's it, I'm making you do overlays next time. We're riding alongside—"

"Nahr Abu Ghurayb," Nguyen says, jostling with the next bump. "The big canal."

Mangler says nothing. Neither does Silver. They bump and jostle in the back of the truck until, at last, it stops right where Silver's GPS says they should.

Silver slips the GPS back into his chest rig and buttons the pouch. "Everyone out."

Insertion in Iraq is never easy—not by the standard of becoming ghosts. In triple canopy jungle, dissolving into the bush would be instant. Stygian 2-3 jumps out the back. Silver slaps the shoulder of the Motor-T Marine who dropped the tailgate, joining the rest of his team as they form a circle in the patch of shadow under the closest berm.

White light had been absent the entire ride. Every driver wore night vision goggles, and as the last of the vehicles creeps past, 2-3 dons their own NVGs. PVS-14s are monocular, leaving one eye to see the world as it really is. That eye has the moon and it has the stars. The convoy's collective silhouette grumbles further east as

Silver works a rock out from under his knee. No one looks at their watch. They are silent; smelling the exhaust in the air, listening to the engines that soon disappear.

Silver holds out a thumbs up. Each team member responds with their own. He waves his hand forward, then points them south.

Not on the map, but there nonetheless, a flimsy bridge gets them over the rushing water. They run across the canal's southern road and make their way down its berm onto flat ground.

Green, that was a fitting word. Silver had been thinking about it since their LT had mentioned the lights. Seeing the world through NVGs meant seeing the world through shades of green and black. Now as much as ever, working clandestine in the wee hours of a hostile land, the familiarity of a palm tree or leaky tractor looked ancient, alien even.

As they head south-southwest, they form a file. Silver walks point, behind him Nguyen, Hutch, then Mangler. They stay close. By day their dispersion could be up to twenty meters. Risk of team-annihilation is absent now, though new dangers have potentially replaced the barrel of a lurking PKM. The team's collective power isn't lost on a man, nor is the thrill of being a lone team, out in the Zaidon, up to no good. As rooftops begin appearing in their NVGs, Silver guides them due west, hoping to save them from the cardinal sin in reconnaissance; being seen. Iraqis would be asleep. Their damn dogs, however, loosely owned, were the bane of covert operations. But none barked for the moment; all the more reason to ensure the night's silence remained.

Silver gives the signal to halt.

"What's up?" Nguyen soon whispers.

Silver is adjusting his NVGs. "Thought I saw something." Silver had studied the map to the point of nausea. It had been so much easier to just follow Ellers. But that era was gone, and he knows that in a minute more, they'd be parallel with their objective. Cast off behind a row of houses sits the farmhouse. He is looking in its direction when

Nguyen asks him again. "Nothing," Silver whispers back, waving them onward. "Let's move."

Before long they see it; a square pile of rubble that had once been a place where people lived. It isn't ideal, but the patch of brush near the farmhouse they make their OP is thick and it is high and reedy, and it allows them to lay flat on their bellies and stare out across the expanse of a neglected field.

"Whatta pile of..." Hutch's voice trails off as Nguyen gets on the radio and informs Higher they've arrived.

Nestled in the weeds with Mangler's SAW covering their six, the team observes. It appears not only was Hutch right, but the house doesn't seem capable of standing up to a strong breeze, let alone enemy activity. The walls had been shot up. The front door had survived, hanging now by a hinge. Only the roof seems to be intact, and that's only because they are too far away to see what hellfire had been brought upon it.

So, Mangler faces away from the house, resting behind his machine gun. Hutch kneels in the shallow ditch that is providing them their weeds.

Nguyen adjusts his NVGs next to Silver. "That's a lot of bullet holes."

Silver zeros in on a patch of wall that had been hit by a MK-19. "You see that blast?"

"...Yep. Do now. Grenade." Nguyen snickers, "This had to be us."

Silver looks closely at a road that ends outside the house's bullet-riddled door. These roads are the type that seem to exist in Iraq only to connect lone hovels to other roads unseen. The thin ribbon of dirt is laid between the house and the field in front of them. On it remain tire tracks. Probably the most boring PowerPoint they'd ever suffered through suddenly proves useful. The road too slim for most vehicles, the tracks too fat to be Datsuns or bongo trucks, the tracks came from Humvees. "And these tracks," Silver whispers. "Whoever shot up the place came rolling in after."

Nguyen takes a long moment, following where Silver directs. "Yeah. I don't—they did this from somewhere behind us. See any shell casings?"

"No, but do *you* see *that*?"

Of course, Nguyen sees it. Hutch sees it too. Light is glowing from behind the mangled door. Every man facing the place flips up their NVGs. The light is sure-as-shit green—*neon*—like a light saber.

"I can't believe it," Silver hears himself say. Now what is left of a window flashes green, then another, so bright Silver sees the look on Mangler's face after he rustles and twists, arriving at Silver's shoulder.

"Someone's in there," Silver says, squeezing his rifle's pistol grip. "Mangler, get back there, brother. Guard our six." Silver hears him slither and now he watches Hutch. Hutch is back on his NVGs, moving his head from left to right. Good, having one man scan for movement freed Silver and Nguyen to put their focus on the house.

A lit backdrop would mean silhouettes. Silver waits to see if a head will pass by a window.

"Dude," Nguyen's tone seems confused. "Radio's down."

Maybe a better team leader would have said something. Silver thinks this and he shakes his head. There are no signs of movement, anywhere, not beyond the door, not in the windows. But the light, it is growing, flashing in bursts as loosened bricks float up from the earth to find holes in the front wall.

"Are you seeing this?"

But Nguyen doesn't answer Silver.

Hutch is whispering erratic and loud. His team leader waves him over.

"Silver," Hutch whispers, crawling on his hands and knees. "Shit's movin'."

Bricks aren't just floating, they are *re*attaching; wedging themselves into the spaces they'd once occupied no different than if hands were doing the fitting.

Bullet holes begin shrinking, disappearing into the strengthening wall. "It's repairing itself," Silver says.

Stygian 2-3 ducks as a bright blast radiates out the door, rolling across the field and over them like a wave. In one instant, all of 2-3's NVGs go down. None know this collective reaction to the rolling wave, only that their own mechanical advantage has abruptly ended. Worried more over the scorn their teammates would surely show them, each man flips their NVGs up, not looking at the other, letting their startled eyes adjust to a night no longer black.

Nguyen slaps Silver's arm with his handset. "You want me to call this brick shit in?" Nguyen puts the handset to his ear. "Sty— goddamn it. Silver, radio's *dead.*"

"What?" Silver gets behind Nguyen, squinting down at the blank screen. It was out—totally dead. All had been charged, from the SINGARs radio on Nguyen's back to the MBITRs on their chests. Silver curses: his MBITR is out, too.

Inner-team comm is doable, voice to voice, but their one and only lifeline to Lieutenant Ashton, the grunts, the artillery that could be called to save them—

—Silver gets down on his knees and unzips Nguyen's butt pack. The spare SINGARS battery is olive drab, same as the radio, both being lit for Silver's naked eyes by unfathomable neon, continuously bursting across the field.

The new battery clicked in, Silver says in Nguyen's ear, "I'm not seeing shit."

"Because it's fucking dead—"

"Y'all seein' this?" Hutch says. His hiss was so urgent it swings every head to the warm bath of white light coming up the farmhouse road.

"Shit," they all seem to say.

A truck is now approaching, a white Iraqi pickup, headlights blazing. The truck clatters and squeaks as its shoddy tires roll it forward.

Silver checks his watch. Its battery has somehow failed them. 1am-something is an odd time for traffic, even if not rolling toward a house lit by an unholy glow. The hair on the back of his neck sparks when the truck accelerates. Only a football field away, the white truck veers off the road, not stopping until its brakes shriek behind the house. Every man in the weeds on the lip of the shallow ditch shoulders his weapon. All battery-powered optics are dead. No longer concealed by the first truck, a second one was following not far behind. And now it approaches. 2-3 knows this isn't good.

Something about Nguyen muttering, "White truck, brown hood", takes Silver's heart out of his throat. This second truck appears exactly that, now skidding to a halt in front of the house. Several men spill out.

"One, two," Silver counts—the driver and passenger are exiting now, every damn one of them armed. "Four, five." All dressed in black, one carries an RPG while the rest hold an arsenal of AKs.

Any enemy bold enough to openly wield a rocket-propelled grenade may be bold enough to use flashlights; something collectively observed as 2-3 hugs the earth and refuses to breathe. Daring to peer out from the defilade, Silver watches as men come from around the back, swarming the front of the house before slinking past the hanging door and disappearing inside.

"There's gotta be a dozen," Nguyen whispers. Mangler then wedges himself between Nguyen and Hutch.

Those who'd gone inside must have been bent on tearing the place apart. Pots clank, what sounds like drawers slam shut. Shouts in Arabic make their way back to 2-3's ears, but none of that noise means a damn thing.

Every Iraqi inside the farmhouse had come from the truck, the first truck; the one that had pulled around back. The second truck, the one that had parked in front of the farmhouse—its occupants were the ones who mattered.

Every enemy who'd dismounted the white truck with the brown hood starts to fan out. Two walk north, vanishing in the direction which 2-3 had originally approached. The one with the RPG is seen for a moment more then he disappears behind the house. And one Iraqi, pressing the buttstock of his AK into his shoulder, is walking right toward them.

5.

11 0118C SEP 05

Whatever the Iraqis are looking for must be eluding them. The green light inside glows on. So does the noise. The light still pours, cracking and pulsing, and the man in his black thobe and piercing eyes is now just a grenade away from Stygian 2-3.

This enemy's satchel hangs loosely over one shoulder, weighted by mags. He points his AK down toward the dry rises of the field. With each step, his face and beard become clearer, until, after a sudden blast of green, he stands before them.

Silver is not the closest. That would be Mangler or Hutch. Like every ditch, their concealment is bordered by the elevation that had been dug up and patted down. At the closer lip, the lip closer to the still-repairing home, the gunman is but a step, casting his eyes beyond them. He steps. Steps then stops, then steps again.

Boom-fwoom-fwoom erupts from Hutch's rifle, tearing holes in the Iraqi's chest before he can scream. Whatever dog may have barked, whatever man may have cried, nothing can be heard. Stygian 2-3 starts dumping mags. Surprise had been on their side, and now it pays. What had remained visible of their enemy was one man, barreling out of the shadows from the north, trying to run inside the house before being shot in the back. The one shouldering the RPG comes out from around the house and slams himself behind the idling truck.

It doesn't take long. Bullets start flying from the house. Windows lit by light don't show shooters but actually conceal them, though Nguyen's 203 round slips in and sends the place into a booming roar.

Silver crawls on his hands and knees, low and fast, away from his team. Gaining the desperately needed dispersion, he rises to a knee and shoulders his rifle.

A sudden blast swings his focus to his immediate left. The other who'd disappeared out to their north had scurried, toward their OP. From behind a mound of dirt a muzzle flashes. Silver's own 203 goes over the flash, but an entire magazine emptied leaves the enemy lifeless. Silver ejects the empty mag, yelling "Changing magazines!" He reloads and turns back to his team right as dragon's breath spews from Mangler. The man with the RPG drops his unfired weapon and slumps against the tailgate. What had been his cover now *dinks* and sings with bullets as glass shatters and tires pop.

Silver's instincts pull him to the radios. This isn't over. As dirt flies off the lip of their ditch his team reloads. They are alone. Now come the windows. Every Marine concentrates on the squares and the open doorway. AKs bark. Frantic cries from inside swell then dissipate. A solitary round comes zinging out, whizzing past Silver's head as he wraps his finger back around his trigger.

When the truck parked around back comes wheeling out, it nearly comes apart over the troughs and rises before landing itself on the road, fishtailing, suffering Mangler's SAW and the team's M4s, due south until it is gone.

"Another one," Nguyen says plain as day.

Inside the farmhouse they are all lathered in the lime neon glow. Stygian 2-3 had entered, cleared each and every room, and in the absence of any living enemy had focused their attention on two of the dead who'd fired at them from a window.

Iraq is the land of gunfights where, save for exceptional circumstances, a fighting team has little way of knowing who shot out the killing round. Never more than the case here. Both men are sprawled on the blood-slicked floor. Death had ripped through their heads, their neck, their black-garbed shoulders. Strange then, that the necklaces around these Muj assholes' necks hadn't suffered a single bullet. Leaning forward, Silver wipes the sweat off his brow and examines the men closely. Definitely necklaces, they appeared to be made of wire and a strung-out display of bone. Out of all the locals they've dealt with, this is a first.

Nguyen, however, isn't concerned with the Iraqis' cheap jewelry. The enemy dead are dressed in black thobes. Their shoddy chest rigs and sandals are common, too. But in the green light's glow, their eyes still seem to be holding a different, undefined type of hate.

Silver watches as Hutch reaches down and fondles a necklace of bone—human bone—frantically wiping his hand on his sleeve.

"These fuckers look straight outta horror movie," Hutch says.

Silver then sees something that prompts him to get his own hands bloody. Pulling down one of the dead's thobes, below a black beard, where collar bones meet chest muscle, are the markings of a tattoo.

"We've got to get S-Two on this," Silver says.

S-2, their battalion's intelligence office, might be able to advise what the hell this tattoo meant. "Guys, check all of them. Tell me if they have a tattoo on their chest."

As his team begins reporting back to him that, in fact, yes, all the dead do, Silver forgets fear and reconnaissance and cosmic confusion and wishes eagerly he could tell Greene. Silver tries his radio. Nothing.

"These fuckin' lights," Silver froths.

The tattoo on each of the dead is the exact thing Greene had drawn. Silver makes more than a mental note then joins the rest of his team.

They search, but here is no definite point from which the light glows. The house itself, its walls, its arches; all seem to permeate. Though fading, what illuminates the team as they rummage through is still strong and bright as any flashlight.

Mangler walks down the one hallway. There'd been a room full of books—a pile that looked to have been getting tossed before he and his boys ruined all the goat-fucker's fun. There'd been another room, too. This one with a lone water bottle laying on the floor. Nothing to write home about except for it was the exact type Marines carried on them or passed out to confused civilians. What had made that room weird—weirder than all the rest—was its far wall. It sported the unmistakable holes of someone's M4, but even those had tricked Mangler's eyes; closing up like a bunch of silenced mouths.

"Whatcha got?" Mangler says over Silver's shoulder.

Silver is on a knee, still kneeling beside one of the dead.

Silver stands up. "Who the fuck knows at this point." In Silver's hands he holds an old-as-hell piece of paper. Something right out of one of those documentaries about King Tut, or something.

Silver looks behind him. He had already been in the book room too. Stuffed in one of the guys' rigs had been this page, stuffed hastily as—

"This may be what they were looking for." He unfolds the find, extending it to the size of a small map, covered from margin to margin with drawings and symbols. Silver flips the paper over and almost gapes.

On the back, surrounded by writing in Arabic, *is* the tattoo—*is* what Greene drew. Only this time the symbol is incased in a florid seal. Its lines squiggly and old, the enshrouding circle puts the figure inside something that looks sort of like a portal.

Silver traces this with the tip of his finger.

At that exact moment, elsewhere in the Zaidon, an imam sets down his book. He closes the book, pressing his hands against his table, sending his chair screeching against bald, polished tile.

The Iraqi is old, but he is not grey. The holy man strokes his beard, casting eyes that have grown wild and lustful toward the open window. He moves, resting his hands on its ledge. A night wind caresses his headdress. Not as in other mosques, where red and whites subdue themselves under the dark rings of a modest agal, his shemagh, hanging low, waves a torpid, somber black.

In this small secret room in the back of an otherwise ordinary mosque, an image hangs on the wall. It is a large, upside-down T, crowned at its top by a hollow circle. On each side are markings. On one is something serpentine, slithering upward from the base. On the other are markings that make the whole thing look like a winged man, facing sideways, holding a curved sword. But this is no drawing, though it matches exactly what Corporal Josh Silver had just traced with his finger. It is a painting. The painting is large, hung on a chain, extending from one lanterned corner to the other. Ink of a long-dried blood, drained from the appropriate sources, slithers and curves and connects on a canvas of skin. Taught on its stretching hooks, it earns the imam's glance before the man departs down a set of stairs.

Outside, the hour grants no noise but the wind. The imam faces the direction of the distant farmhouse, then he raises his arms. He begins to chant, calling forth sounds no sleeping neighbor can know. The winds blow his thobe and his shemagh, wrapping him as the night becomes a sweltering gale.

6.

11 0606C SEP 05

"You expect me..." the groggy company commander declares, waving his hand at the other staff seated at the table. "You expect *us*, Corporal Silver, to actually believe that?"

Oppressing the room is also Lieutenant Ashton, their silent platoon sergeant, and the first sergeant in charge of all Stygian platoons. On the other side of the company office, backs against the wall, is Stygian 2-3, looking down at their boots. "You're gonna try to pull the wool over everyone's eyes and stick to every single radio went down, and all at once?"

"Sir," Silver sighs. He looks up from the cement, glancing at the gold maple leaf on the company commander's collar before looking him in the eye. "I know how crazy it sounds, but all our radios—even my watch—everything went down when—"

"When what, Corporal?" the major snarls. "When creepy lights 'faded away'?"

The green lights had faded away, not long after the fire fight, restoring every piece of gear beholden to a battery. Higher was now busy solidifying their zero-casualties gunfight into a tall tale about not charging radios. That version died when Lieutenant Ashton dared remind the major that they did, in fact, call everything in—just woefully late. The new working theory was team negligence.

Lieutenant Ashton looks at the team. "Corporal Nguyen?"

Outside, Camp Fallujah is awakening with the crackling of dawn. Motors grumble, platoons of admin types and diesel mechanics run by the office's windows, calling out cadence as every other member in 2-3 creaks their neck toward their radio operator.

Nguyen is still staring at the toe of his boot. "Sir," he says. He takes a deep breath. "Sir, it was our fault."

"You kiddin' me, man?"

Mangler knuckles Hutch's thigh, cutting short whatever their junior-most was about to go full foot-in-mouth over.

The company commander stands up. "Silver, next time you are outside the wire, your radios better be fuckin' charged. All of them. And you better be hopping on the line if you heroes go and get compromised again. And *don't* give me shit about a watch—that's like some PFC saying he can't call in after a ninety-six because a satellite's down. We'll pass up the tattoo thing."

"Aye, sir." Silver looks down at his notepad. *bricks. Repairing?? Saw the green !* He'd scribbled and circled it all twice. He stuffs the notepad back in his pocket, along with any hope of being believed.

7.

```
11 0713C SEP 05
```

Before its translation to Greek, the Necronomicon had been titled by its mad author the *Kitab al-Azif.* Originating in the Arabic world, offshoots had immediately sprouted, trickling down from Damascus and spreading into the heart of the Abbasid Caliphate. Of all who worshipped in secret, those branded by the mark were the fiercest: a pernicious sect—*the* Sect—who conquered or converted all others, leaving now a lone cult; worshippers of the vilest evil, waiting as their cleric cast a finger to the wind; waiting for the maligned heavens and putrescent earth to deliver them their master.

In a small village, no more than a mile from that dreaded farmhouse, those who'd escaped the fire of Stygian 2-3 slide their truck to a halt against a random house as the same CAAT Team who'd shot up Sergeant Miller closes in.

The fighters, branded and armed, jump out from behind a shot-up tailgate to make their last stand.

Those who remained of the botched farmhouse expedition were driving back to report to their imam. He'd sensed the glorious disturbance Miller had unwittingly caused. *Growing.* Calling his greater ear like insects on the wind. The Sect had been furtive in Iraq for decades, even centuries. Miller's summoning in the farmhouse had alerted the Sect; expediting their ambitions. Unbeknownst to the Americans, the imam's fighters had found two pages—more pages—loosed from the *Al-Azif* and discovered wedged between books Miller or Ortiz hadn't cared to tear. One found was a big page, the size of a sprawled out Quran, but had been inexcusably left behind, even though its possessor had become a martyr during their battle with crusaders who'd been cowardly lying in wait.

But before the survivors could get to the mosque, the Sect's centuries old cover, they'd turned a sharp corner, crazed by the excitement and fear that surely pursued them, and ran head-on into a vehicle check point.

Throwing the truck in reverse, they littered the place with shell casings as startled grunts and field MPs scramble behind Humvees. What ended up being the entire AO's radio chatter, unit after unit was kept from the MEK's 9/11 anniversary breakfast, keeping instead their eyes open all morning for a lone white pickup, full to the brim with black-clad killers.

It was the CAAT Team who'd gotten lucky, on routine patrol when some hawk-eye in a turret saw the ass end of the truck sticking out from behind a pump house. So went the chase, ending at a row of wobbling huts now exploding with gunfire and Iraqis trying to escape.

The house is small; chipping apart as rounds lacerate its walls. MK-19 grenades thud against the white truck outside, blasting off a door and sending in every direction freed, flying metal. A woman, covered from head-to-toe in blue, is laid flat after screaming out from the front door. No prayers protected her from the bullet that punched through her chest, blackening her garment as a member of the Sect sprays fire out behind her.

There is an American Humvee for every Sect fighter. As the five vehicles crawl to engulf their targets in the inescapable shape of an L, a Sect member—bleeding from his mouth—charges out the rear, fumbling an AK twice before losing his brains to a tracer out the long barrel of a .50 cal.

When the same machine gun opens up a hole in the wall, from the crumbling blackness fires out an RPG. The grenade screams past the .50, exploding against the next vehicle's turret. The stunned gunner's sunglasses fly off in the smoke and skin and bright whines of iron on steel. He looks where his hands had been; red and pink nubs, about to bleed. No Marine dismounts. They lay into their crew-served, unable to hear dying cries. In a matter of minutes all in the house are shredded and dead. Except one.

A lone fighter clutches the other page they'd found in the farmhouse. Unable now to ever give it to his leader, shot and bleeding, he angrily reads. Even the strict hierarchy of the Sect could not sway him. He'd read the words, knowing the incantation he now spit and uttered were penned with the grim design of cheating death. The last rite spoken, the paling man lays his head in a pool of blood. His eyes do not shut, though through them he no longer sees.

8.

`11 1917C SEP 05`

When night appears over Iraq, never does the starlight blanket the world greater. What had been the betraying grandeur of autumn enshrouds the destroyed home.

A girl is in the house. Neck arched and mouth wide, she is laying where she fell. Someone's gun had ripped away the side of her head, causing a ten-year-old brain to leave its bone encasement in tiny chunks that have turned grey. She is in the main room, in the same congealing pool as the lone fighter who'd read the blasphemous page.

Dogs bark. Insects, uncommon in this part of the reddened map, flutter and trill. The preternatural chorus rings through the ear of no one as the girl's fingers begin to twitch.

When her eyes pop, they do so with an open pure light. Green and radiating, they serve her well as she stands and brushes herself free of clots and debris.

She walks over and pries from the fighter's stone hand the parchment, lighting it in lime when she stares down on familiar runes before folding it neatly, stuffing the page in the pocket of her girlish trousers.

In what remains of a mirror, through its shards her lit eyes stare back. She does not cringe. Nor does she smile. The girl's clothes will work. Black trousers. Black blouse, hanging loose. Blood will dry. She walks to where *she'd* died and picks up what had been her brother's kufi. She puts on the brimless, rounded cap, tucking in flaps of superfluous flesh, hiding long hair and the mortal head wound as she leisurely walks out the door.

Met by the bugs and a piece of the moon, the girl surveys what a gunfight has left. Casings from paltry weaponry lay strewn, some places in heaps near the tracks of the departed human vehicles. The creature—the child—this summoned servant of a great evil well-aware of Iraq bends down to pick up a pair of sunglasses. What or whomever may have been watching from behind berm or wall would soon only witness the sudden departure of her eyes' blaze. The child laughs—a deep, unearthly cackle—levitating the plastic glasses above her open palm before putting them on.

Beyond power lines, hanging low and still, behind the tops of distant trees awaits a very useful human. The imam is calling her, howling from his open window.

The dirt path the child strides down will take her to a new village. Traversing fields, snaking between low walls, the high wooden doors of a mosque will greet her soon. Those within care nothing for the pathetic religions stupefying the deserts with tales of various messiah. Inside she will be much more than welcomed.

High above the day's carnage floats Sergeant Paul Miller. He rests in the breeze, unseen, blighting out the light of stars. He flies across the radar-sensitive sky. Miller knows he'll have but a moment, a moment to soar, to seek, then comes his old side's inspection. Mysterious objects moving above battle spaces made for puzzled commanders then curious pilots—hastening his tattered, sweat-stained gown to wave and flap when the time came to swoop down and hide. Hiding under trucks has thus far worked, so has the concealment provided by weed-ridden canals. He has flown, he has hidden, and he is not done.

Slung over each of his shoulders are satchels, overflowing with bread—peeled from unattended ovens—stolen bottles of water, magazines off his most recent kill. In each hand he holds an AK by their wooden grips. Their old owners forgoing their usefulness when he strangled them with a delightful summoning of an adroit tentacle.

His eyes now permanently, dementedly, hopelessly wild, he scratches a rifle's metal fire selector against his hairy chin. Miller watches as the child strolls merrily toward the black bulk of a distant minaret.

9.

`12 0950C SEP 05`

"You son of a—" Silver grunts, tightening his headlock. Nguyen scrapes at Silver's eyes and belts him in the gut with a fist. The two keep at it, trading blows as they twist and curse and snarl.

Save for specks of blood, the team room is white and particle-board brown; plastered by walls of maps and turned claustrophobic by hanging weaponry and ammo cans on the floor on which their boots scuff and squeak as Hutch tries to pry them apart. Sergeant Greene's presence is now entirely unnoticed—though his barging in to pass on the latest news is what sent them swinging. Greene charges, his head down, latching onto Nguyen. "Newjin, stop—stop it!" Hutch almost eats Silver's right hook as all four go toppling over an ammo crate.

When the door swings open Hutch looks up at Mangler.

"Shit," Mangler tosses his Nalgene bottle and grabs the first available camouflage. "E—", with the combined effort of Greene and Hutch and Mangler, Silver and Nguyen are separated, "—nough!"

"Jesus." Greene breathes.

"You piece of shit," Silver says, red as hell, wiping his lip.

"Fuck you!" Nguyen is panting. He straightens and eyes Hutch. "Fuck all you."

"Hey," Hutch shrugs. "It's whatever, man."

Mangler looks at Greene.

"It's not about what they will or won't believe, Nguyen." Silver says, catching his breath. Mangler's still sweaty from his run, but it's Silver who's still breathing hard. Silver grabs a water bottle. "It's about what *is* and what fuckin' *isn't*."

Nguyen scoffs.

"Those lights were real," Hutch says. "LT sent us out because of 'em. They—"

"Real shmeal," Nguyen won't look at his team. "Doesn't mean shit, Hutch. Yeah lights—but I don't wanna hear about that devil bullshit."

"What the hell else could it be then? We all saw."

Greene gives a curious glance at Hutch. "You all saw what?"

Silver slides past Mangler and shuts the door. "Now that the *team's* all here, start over, Greene. Tell us again."

Nguyen laughs, a dry hollow laugh exempt of humor. "Yeah," he says. "If there's anyone else who'll think this shit is stupid it'll be Mangler."

"Man, I can leave. It ain't—"

"No, Greene." Hutch bars the door.

"Yeah" The Mangler plops down on a can. "What'd you say that started all this?"

What Greene had been listening to for the past few hours he could still hardly believe. His radios had lit alive with such chaotic fury he'd reasoned some twisted joke had spun out of control. Put into the wrong ears, and at the right time, the Marine Corps had taught him even the most far-reaching rumors could grow legs. He'd come to let Silver in on the joke—not that he'd really appreciate the irony. Silver had seen that damn sketch. But Silver, like every other cowboy inside the MEK, wouldn't understand how that drawing and what was humming up and down the comm lines could be connected. That was before Greene had watched the team react.

"All right," Greene says, slowly, looking around at the other four like one would pounce if he dared speak with any enthusiasm. "So, I've been monitoring all morning. Apparently a new, and I mean *lethal*, terror cell has emerged. A grunt platoon got obliterated around sunrise. Sucks, I know, but what's crazier is all the Iraqis. A fuck ton of 'em, too. Shot. Burned. Other shit that's makin' no sense. One phone kept sayin' Muj fighters got taken out too—no, it wasn't the grunts. Apparently, they'd checked. It's this new cell, man. I thought it was bullshit until about an hour ago."

"Silver." Lieutenant Ashton stands in the doorway. "Sergeant Greene?" The officer takes his eyes off the crypto-linguist and nods at Silver. "When you're done, come see me."

"Roger, sir," Silver says, sitting back down and looking up at Greene. The door smacks shut.

"...CIA," Greene continues. "They hit us up. Something about this cell having a super young-ass leader and then they mentioned something about..." He tries not to look at Nguyen but can't help it. "Somethin' about green lights."

There it was, what had sparked the fight. Mangler doesn't react, but Hutch does. "I'm with my TL."

"Of course you are," Nguyen shakes his head and leans against a table.

Silver says nothing, but his heart warms as Hutch speaks. "Bro," Hutch says to Nguyen. "We should go back. That's all."

"You think I'm afraid to go back?"

"I do," Mangler says, chuckling as Nguyen flips him off.

Hutch tries to speak but Silver is on his feet. "No, Nguyen. Not in the slightest. I get why you stuck to your story, and you're right, they won't believe shit, other than we fucked up." Nguyen pries his stare away and preoccupies himself with a stain of gunk on the floor. He chews on his tongue, making motions like rolling something around in his mouth. Silver walks over to a shelf where he keeps folders and laminates for route overlays. "Here," he says to Greene, unfolding the page he took off the dead fighter. He hands it over.

Greene takes one look at the symbol of the Sect—*the* symbol—then looks up at Silver.

"Yeah," Silver says.

The other Marines watch as Greene repositions his glasses then scrutinizes the Arabic scrawled amongst the runes.

"Hey," Hutch says to Nguyen. "You know how you always tell me about the history of Recon? I'm thinkin' this is somethin' right up that alley."

Mangler is beginning to show the first signs of boredom. Silver's focus is intently on Greene.

Nguyen pushes himself off the table's edge. "This," he says, giving away some deep, unacknowledged intuition by pointing at: "Silver's pirate map...we aren't exactly talking reporting bottom samples."

"Agreed," says Silver. "But this is info gathering at its finest. A mystery. We need to go back."

"This time let's capture one of those fucks," Mangler says, making the hair on Silver's arms spark. "*Alive.*"

Silver stiffens further as Greene, who'd been staring down at the confiscated page, peels away from the words to strafe him with the first serious look he'd ever given.

"You guys do that," Greene says, "bring an interpreter."

"Why?" seemingly coming from everyone.

"I hate to say it like this, but you don't know how much time you'll have. This here," he waves the page then slowly hands it back. "It isn't Islam. Whoever this new terror cell is, they aren't talking, not on phones. Not anymore. We'd have caught it by now. The shit I'm hearing is freaking out normal Muj. IED-planters, bomb-makers, they're all sayin' the same."

"Which is what, Greene?" Silver is still.

"That whatever's going on out there might be the worst shit this war has seen. Y'all hero it out there, y'all catch one of 'em, everybody from General Mattis to motherfuckin' me is gonna be beatin' down your door."

"Let's fucking do it then." Nguyen couldn't have said anything better. Looking at Silver, "Think LT will let us?"

"Don't know," Silver says, slapping Greene on the shoulder as he heads for the door. "But I'm going to find out."

###

"Going back to a compromised OP isn't exactly standard operating procedure," the LT says. Left over from the last unit that occupied the honeycombs of what is now 5th Recon's headquarters, Lieutenant Ashton's lawn chair squeaks as he adjusts to take in his being-talked-about team leader. Of the three team leaders in Stygian 2-3, Silver had quickly managed to insert himself as the target for gossip.

"Sir, about the radios."

"I don't give a shit about the radios." The young lieutenant, crisp-eyed and hawk-nosed, clam-shells his laptop and gives Silver his full attention; squinting at the TL's bloodied lip then shaking his head. "You guys each deserve a Bronze Star. If it wasn't for this Hearts and Minds crap, I'd of had every one of those fuckos you killed strapped to the hood of a Humvee and brought back here and dumped on the floor." Lieutenant Ashton had wanted to speak with him it seemed. To the surprise of no one in 2-3, and now Sergeant Greene, the platoon commander had put together the reports. "So those lights," he says. "They're real? You saw them?"

"Yes, sir. We all did."

Lieutenant Ashton points to a map taped to the wall. Silver had already noticed the bewilderment of circles markered on its surface. "That's every infantry unit, SF unit and sniper team that'll be out tonight. As you may possibly be the highest-ranking who's actually seen some of this, I wanted to ask you, if I were to prepare an additional report, what would you want to see in it."

It was like turning on a fire hose. Silver unloads, from green light to floating bricks to practically pushing the symbol-haunted paper against the LT's face. The lieutenant takes hold of the odd bit of evidence, turning it this way and that.

"You know there were cases," the LT says, "in Vietnam." He rests both of his elbows on the table and leans forward. "Hell, even up in Fort Story during patrol week—exhausted guys reporting sightings that aren't actually there." Silver cringes, remembering his bearing as he feels the LT's trust in his words continue to slip. "In rare cases, multiple. Hallucinations no doubt, and no doubt coming from lack of sleep. Now I know that's not your case, but I'm advising you not to mention any more of the stuff you just did. Lights are one thing. We're not trying to convince the colonel of magic."

Silver remembers a disposable camera he has tucked away. "Roger that, sir."

The lieutenant looks Silver up and down. At parade rest, he stood like someone competent and the furthest from insane. "You got anything else?"

"Yes, sir…I do." He is given back the damn paper, trying what is probably the vainest attempt in concealing its importance as he creases it back into a square and slides it deep into his pocket. "We need to go back. Back to that farmhouse."

The LT sighs, scratching his high-reg hair. At last, he says, "There's an uprising in the Zaidon. I do think it's related to the men you put down. This is me risking my neck here, but I'll run it up the chain and see if we can get you approved. Silver, no fucking up on this one."

"You got it." Silver goes for the door, unsure whether he is excited or afraid. He turns, "Sir?"

"Yeah?"

"Can we get an interpreter?"

10.

`13 0004C SEP 05`

They'd slept the day away, as best they could. Rigger's tape and cardboard had been working as blinds, but blackout did little to prevent the penetration of yelling shitheads, off-day Stygians barging in to be cast out and cursed, or the thunderous boom of howitzers, awakening and reawakening, answering calls of men already negotiating whatever the hell may be out there.

Stygian 2-3 slept, then they didn't, then a watch's alarm pulled them up from half-dreams and into their gear.

Four minutes after midnight, the team and one terrified interpreter—or 'terp, as is commonly said—begin climbing into Humvees provided by the motor pool. Each equipped with a driver and turret-gunner, the two vehicles are loaded.

Lead vehicle: driver, turret gunner, Silver sitting front passenger, the interpreter directly behind him and Hutch behind their driver.

The rear vehicle goes driver, turret gunner, Nguyen front passenger, an empty rear passenger seat and Mangler; slapping his SAW, looking at their gunner's legs.

The main gate is soon behind them. In a matter of a few spins, both vehicles depart the asphalt, cruising under the power lines and then the lefts and rights and curving sways before their reintroduction with torn up patches of ill-fitting road. Every man but the interpreter watches through night vision as the minimalist of convoys descends southward.

"Ready for this, TL?" Mangler says over the MBITRs.

Silver says nothing. His mind is on the mission. There was no way Battalion would have signed off on another observation post. One compromised position was enough. A more direct approach had surprisingly won over the higher ups. They are going to slither up to the house and raid the damn thing. If enemy are present— good. If not, they will setup on the roof, hoping enemy will return, allowing them to whoop it on and, hopefully, capture a prisoner. One of those Recon Diary books talked about how they'd done a capture in Nam, and as Silver watches the road begin its slip under the hard packed dirt—

Silver doesn't know what happens. His consciousness, the thing he defines as "Silver," the collection of memories and thoughts, goes right out behind his wind. It, Silver, flies out his mouth, up at the ceiling and then comes floating down and Silver goes back in.

An explosion had ripped to life outside his door, bringing chunks of dirt and road onto the vehicle's hood. The blast had brought with it flame and the concussion had turned off his NVGs. He turns his vision back on then flips them off his face to watch the knuckled hands of their driver pulling their steering wheel a hard left.

"IED!" the turret-gunner yells.

Silver knew. They'd rolled off the hardball and in that moment the tire by his feet had taken the brunt of an improvised explosive device. Both vehicles halt. 2-3 pours out.

"Stay right here," Silver tells their interpreter, a skinny mustached Iraqi who nods energetically at the command.

The smell of burned rubber fills Silver's nostrils as he joins Hutch, pushing out to pull security. In these moments it was foundational to believe whomever had planted the IED had done so with the intent of initiating an ambush. Though the Muj rarely fought at night, this new group had, and Silver can't help but crack a smile when he sees Nguyen and the Mangler disappear behind their own Humvee, completing a three-sixty perimeter as both turret-gunners swing the barrels of their machine guns north-south.

A voice crackles in Silver's headset. Nguyen says, *"Battalion wants to know damage."*

"Roger. Wait one." Of course Higher would be rattled. Only two damn Humvees—something nobody liked, and only a striking shortage of available convoys and Ashton's insistence to let his guys "Get back on the horse" finally allowed for such a risk. But now it had come back to bite them. They were practically alone, and with a compromised vehicle.

Like most roads here, the packed dirt ribboned atop diggings of earth that had once been the contents of canals and trenches dug out by generations. Silver had descended the low berm to peer out into the beginning of fields. Climbing back, he walks over to where their rear tire had narrowly escaped. Their driver, who'd been quick, meets him at the crater.

"Fancy drivin', Tex."

"Third one this fuckin' month," the driver spits, adjusting his NVGS, staring down at the hole. *"Look* at that mother."

Silver does. This size, and at this time of night; all signs pointed to a pressure-plate. IEDs wired to lurking cell phones could be big— Humvee-flipping big. But pressure-plate IEDs were the ones that ripped tanks a new ass. This one had blasted its hellish load away from them, exchanging what would've been certain death for the shredded stink of a front passenger tire.

"Corporal," the driver says. "Lend me a man so we can change this tire? Already checked. Axle's fine."

Silver gets on his MBITR, calling Hutch over and giving Nguyen a report back for Higher. He reassumes security down off the road as a jack gets pulled and wedged underneath.

The two work silently enough, though there is no sparing the night from the sound of a lug wrench twisting, the lugs dropping and thudding into a helmet resting in the dirt. Noise goes out over the land, stiffening Silver's spine when a door slams needlessly. What a fool he felt, concerned over a candle's worth of sound when terror the size of a shrieking sun had just flown, low and loud, across the blackened world that he swears is now staring back at him.

He turns and he squints. Through his NVGS, Hutch and their driver are tearing the mangled tire free. He turns back to reface the night as they unstrap the spare, letting the mammoth bounce off the back before rolling it past the innermost reach of the blast's crater, up to the naked hub.

What made every horror movie involving guns so damn stupid was the exact tool he'd been holding coolly with both hands. Weapons, and lots of them, didn't make for tripping women or small kids with special powers—found at just the right time. Guns meant safety. What lethal force could be rattled by the axe murderer? What trained team of Recon Marines could be in danger in a shadow-haunted night where he felt in his marrow things were crawling their way? A gust of wind licks his face, and maybe that is what makes him shiver.

"Guys," Hutch soon says over the MBITRs. "Truck's good."

"We rollin'?" Mangler's voice comes on.

Silver bites his lip. They aren't far from that flimsy little bridge. They could set out from here. "Yeah," Silver says. "Let's load up."

The blast and its flame had alerted everyone within a mile. Perhaps a better leader would soon practice greater caution. Pulling back to the MEK would certainly be exemplary of that. But confidence in their ability to hide in shadow and move out on foot into silent wastes only doubled a burgeoning, unsettling curiosity. Regardless of Nguyen's denial, Manger's seeming indifference and a growing religious fervor coming from Hutch, in Silver smoldered some faceless desire. That farmhouse, it was near, and something had to be there.

Back in their seats, the men's teeth chatter as the trucks surmount a stretch of potholes. Soon they make their hard left. Silver tells the driver to gun it, then, after a furious stretch, they are dismounting once more. In front of them flows the Nahr Abu Ghurayb canal.

Without a word the Humvees kick up dust and are gone. Stygian 2-3 and their interpreter make for the bridge, running across its planks and ending in a circle down on the flat ground.

"Terp," Silver hisses. "Over here."

Whereas every Marine takes a high knee and statues in silence, their attachment is on both knees, outside the circle. Not his fault his lack of night vision was rendering him a shivering puppy, but his mumbling is destroying their crucial ritual of stop, look, listen, smell. He heeds Silver, crawling on his hands and knees past an amused Hutch and Mangler, coming up to smother their team leader like a backpack. Silenced, he forgoes taking his hand off Silver's shoulder as the team now listens.

No cars or rattling bongos. Under bright stars is very much the world that had met them two nights prior. Silver holds out his thumb. Each and every team member responds with their own. He waves his hand, then points the team south.

Their file is patently Silver, Nguyen, Hutch, Mangler—only now with Terp walking clumsily behind their leader. Familiar rooftops appear, looming larger as they trek over the fields. Not only no cars or bongo trucks, but not a single barking dog. It had become the stuff of lore; how after any action on any particular crinkle on the map there appeared the roving patrols of those damnable mutts. Not one being out surprises Silver, but only as they see the approaching, unlit dullness of their objective does it occur to him not only this alarming reality, but, far stranger is—

"Dude..." someone says.

Behind the row of roofs and down the old road loomed the farmhouse. Not a man among them hadn't been looking over the dashboard along the way, half-expecting to see a fireworks display of lime they'd have to explain to their drivers. There hadn't been any light, nor is there now. What stands before them is a farmhouse, built to perfection. No bullet had scarred the whitish plaster. Not a loose brick lay about the dirt, still carved by the tracks of truck tires.

"What the?" Mangler says.

Hutch pulls out his dog tags, now including a dangling crucifix. He closes his hand around the cross then stuffs it all back behind his armor.

Nguyen says nothing. Dithering is their 'terp as Silver's eyes grow wide.

11.

13 0118C SEP 05

Despite the enchanted exterior, what lay inside was the same as last time.

The same except for that not one body laid dead on the floor. Blood is still there; dried streaks the team first noticed upon making entry, streaks that led to the front door and disappear at the sand. Given the rearranged appearance that had stopped them in their tracks, a second survey of the rooms and subordinate clutter now demands their utmost scrutiny.

By way of the front door, they are again met by the wings of a T-shaped hallway. To one's left the hall ends dumbly at the face of a wall. Proceeding forward though takes them through an open area, too bare to be called a living room, ordained with only a wooden door on its left wall that opens inward to a lone bedroom. Further on, the space transforms into something like a kitchen, equipped with the place's rear door, then ends at a spiral staircase bound for the flat, low roof. But as his guys flow through the farmhouse, securing each and every space as they'd done countless times in stateside shoot houses, Silver's eyes are on the right wing of the T. Two doorless rooms await; the first owning no more than an estranged water bottle, the second disrupted by a now-calm storm of torn books and tattered, balled-up pages.

Silver looks beyond his following Terp and gives an approving thumbs up to Nguyen. Nguyen and Mangler are headed for the roof, soon to be followed by Silver and Hutch.

"Nothin' new, brother," Hutch soon appears around a corner. "You want me down here?" Silver waves him off, listening as Hutch's boots go clopping up the stairs.

Silver doesn't expect to find anything. Not really. If the Muj hadn't run off with all the juicy whatever, chances were high the normal, post-gunfight Iraqis would have crawled in and picked the place clean.

"Sir," the interpreter says in Silver's ear, clearing his throat. "Sir, do I go upstairs?" Interpreters were a mixed bag. Some hailed from as far as Sudan. Most, right here in Iraq. Some were meek and squeamish while others chomped at the bit to help smack around detainees and petitioned platoon leadership for their own M4.

"Terp," as he was called, was of the meeker sort. They'd wanted Omar, the Sudanese Muslim the teams all reverently referred to as MC Hammer. But Hammer was already out with another group, destining 2-3 to this pipe-brush of a man. But he wasn't bad. Just nervous, fidgeting from the sort of insecurity children exhibit when exposed to all things new. "No," Silver says, leading them into the book room. "You hang by me."

Silver is looking through the books. Last time the lights came seemingly unprovoked—*seemingly*. No things come without reason. Something was causing the phenomenon. He scours for clues.

"Sir," Terp says again. "Maybe I will—"

"Stay *right* here." Silver tosses another book, moving to a fresh pile. If he could summon whatever was brewing, whatever had rebuilt the house, surely it would mean the arrival of those new fighters. Silver liked their odds. Greene can say all he wants, enough time in recon left all in it painfully aware of the indulgence those who sat glued to radios poured into the most paltry and static of reports. A few new drums for Mangler's SAW and a bushel of frag grenades should be enough. They'd beat superior numbers before, right outside, in a godforsaken ditch. From the protection and elevation of a roof they could rain down hellfire and brimstone. But first they had to summon their targets.

Summon, Silver laughs—fixated on the word. Yes, he wishes to attract those tattooed shitheads, and yes, they'd probably come rolling in after the light show, if he could make it happen. But, he concedes as he tosses another book and unwads a random page off the floor, the enemy isn't what ultimately interests him. Even a captured prisoner would be but a conduit, one to pry, determinedly hoping to learn what powers were at work.

The room lights ablaze. Something he'd touched, something he'd activated just turned the room into a searing…orange? Terp is sucking bright the cherry of a freshly light cigarette. He's leaning against the wall, still putting away his lighter. The sheer lack of light discipline sends Silver charging. "Do *not* do that again," Silver froths. "Put that shit out."

Terp apologizes and snuffs out his smoke, hanging his head.

"Damn," Silver breathes, retreating back to the books. What could those fighters have wanted? It was as if—*the page!* Silver unzips a pouch near his pistol. Scanning the Arabic, "Wait" he says. "Hey, can you read this?"

Nguyen's voice sounds in Silver's headset. "Just made our comm window with Higher."

"Roger." Silver pays no mind to anything but what's in his hands. He unfolds the page he took off the fighter here, in this house, moving to the one window of the book room. White light defied covert operations. There was enough moon to read. He pulls Terp next to him and then hands him the paper.

Terp sees quickly what Greene had seen. Plain, bald Arabic streaming under and over drawings he does not like at all. Odd for his native tongue, many nominal sentences all shared one reoccurring quirk. A space making no sense had been used to separate what seemed to be the end of one phrase and the beginning of a smaller, related other. He chooses one at random and reads it out loud.

Silver looks at every corner. Hoping to see light, or even a floating book like the bricks, he sees only Terp.

"What's wrong?" Silver asks. The interpreter isn't looking at him, but past him, out the window. Silver had seen fear. It crippled men. Bore others useless until their harder selves pulled them up and out of blood-soaked terror. But this, this look, the Iraqi stutters and shakes, beyond fear, gripping the page he'd read with frozen hands, as if one loosened finger would send him hurling, wailing out into space.

Silver spins, then he sees it.

Behind him it had appeared. Out in the night, not a grenade's toss from the window, stands something Silver's eyes are struggling to realize.

This, he thinks.

This is—

This is insanity!

Larger than a Humvee—larger than a damn tank—taller than the house he cowers in, a thing is out there. Silver shoulders his rifle but he does not fire. He is on a knee, looking up as a dragon flexes its membranous wings. At the end of the dragon's neck, high above the roof, a lurching long head stares up, to a place beyond the house, beyond reason itself.

It all then happens at once: Terp's bright scream, the monster's mouth opens, and every gun on the roof comes alive.

Glass flies as Silver blasts through the window. There is no way that he missed. Bullet after bullet enters the dragon, who gives back nothing but teeters and an uninterested twist. Above Silver, more than one mag is changing. The SAW sprays. A grenade comes down and explodes under the forelimbs of the gargantuan.

It reacts; crying more irksome than mouth-caught razors. But so, even fighting losing one's eardrums and eyes needling to near panic, Silver can't help but think, in an instant, the foul thing had jumped back not because of the blast's damage, but only because the noise of the grenade's sudden boom.

It doesn't attack them, and it doesn't fly away.

It stands, digging its claws into the dirt. Silver becomes aware of his heartrate. What has he done? He breathes, and he breathes again, training his sights between the thing's eyes. A crack of the rifle does it. Everything has a spot. Body armor doesn't cover all of a man, Humvees are unhinged by blasts from below, and whatever from Hell itself he'd put down owned a head no less vulnerable than the sickened horse it resembled.

When the dragon falls over, its clawing limbs catch the other in a clumsy trip, sending the beast down as firing Marines watch it crawl into a ball. Bullets penetrate a slimy, reptilian hide—though the onslaught does little as it presses its bat-like wings against the earth. Slowly the beast rises, not standing but ending in a languid splay, intent on staring up at the night.

"Terp!" Silver spins and yells at their interpreter, splayed out on the floor, much like the dragon.

Now Silver hears his men. "It's movin'!" Nguyen's voice cuts through brick.

Silver pulls his eyes off the 'terp's frantic, flailing arm just in time to watch the dragon's wing also flap and stretch. Gunfire continues, but not from Silver. "Did you trip?" he asks, bewildered, and for a different reason. Looking beyond the window and back to Terp, back and forth like a maniac, Silver then sees. "Get up!" He runs over, grabbing Terp by his collar, hoisting the man back up onto his feet.

And, too, the monster is now standing.

"Cease!" Silver screams into his MBITR. "Cease fire!"

In an instant his team is down there. Outside, dogs are now in a sustained frenzy as the smell of gunpowder fills the crowded room.

"Are you crazy?!" Mangler looks at Silver then out past the shards of the window.

"Watch," Silver says, not sure if he believes it. He grabs Terp by his collar again, this time kicking his legs out from under him.

"Noooo," Mangler oaths. "No freakin' way." Hutch and Nguyen clutch their rifles and run to the window. The beast had toppled to the earth.

"What the—" Nguyen turns to Silver, watching as his TL helps the Iraqi back up. "What's going on?" The beast, the dragon—this thing is regaining its clawed footing, rising as if a puppet pulled taut on invisible strings. "There's no fucking way I'm ever calling this in."

Silver looks at his wrist. His watch still works.

"Terp," Hutch says. "What the fuck is that thing?"

The bewildered Iraqi only mutters more questions, staring fearful at Silver, not shrugging free of the Marine's grip.

"I don't know," Silver says. "But I think we control it."

"No," Hutch points at Terp. "I think *he* does."

"This is not good," Terp says in English. "We should not be here, doing this, in this evil house of farm. Look here," he fingers a point on the page. "It is saying there are portals." He hands Silver back his blasphemy, prompting Nguyen to peer up out the window as the beast's winged arm moves in accordance.

Nguyen hesitates. Every man watches as he reaches for his radio's handset, soon placing his fingers back on his weapon. "I don't think it's going to hurt us."

"Man is your boy Greene ever gonna freak." Mangler slaps Silver's ass.

Odd, but Nguyen's words seem to penetrate deep. Every patrol they'd been on, Iraqi attachments treated the guidance of Americans with a reluctant form of reverence. Stygian 2-1 had once convinced Hammer that no MREs contained any real meat, mirthfully pulling back at the last moment a spoonful of pork from the Muslim's opening mouth. Little different now with Terp, for his eyes had lost all fear, replaced with a growing childlike gleam. Terp not only flaps his arms, delighting as the monster responds, but he fills Silver with a million ideas when he gleefully states "the demon" may take his commands.

"Don't you even think about it, Silver," Hutch says.

Silver is at the window. "See if it'll fly."

No more than a word spreads those mammoth wings, kicking up flumes of dirt and dust as the beast shoots skyward.

"Holy shit!" Mangler says. "We're riding this thing back to the MEK!"

Hutch is less amused. He'd hoped Nguyen's patent skepticism would hold true, but now that's one more thing that is gone.

"Bring it back down," Silver says to Terp.

Every man but Hutch crowds at the window, still gawking, moving their heads in unison as Terp mumbles new words.

"Wait—where is it?"

"There!"

Hutch, unable to resist, wedges himself between Silver and Terp just in time to see the shimmering outline of damnation itself begin to fade. And when it did, it kept fading; hovering just above its bedeviled launch site before all were staring through an ethereal corpus.

"It's gone," Nguyen whispers. "It just...fizzled out."

"What is that?" the interpreter gasps, looking behind them, out into the hall. Green light is back, pulsing somewhere outside the room.

Silver wastes no time. In the hallway, he is washed over as the adjacent room—

the room, unbeknownst to him, where Miller executed the second summoning and where the homeowner had been devoured, blooms. The room shimmers, empty save for the glowing, growing light; creeping along the wall by way of two ends, forming what is slowly becoming a circle.

Silver thinks of that drawing, the tattoos—the portal-like ring and what is depicted in its center. Nothing is inside the still-forming ring but the barrenness of the brick beyond, and though only Terp has new reason to stammer and fear, every man inside now watches in silence as the circle draws itself complete.

Silver follows his instincts, keying his MBITR. He gets nothing. He looks: his watch is out.

"Radio's toast," Nguyen then says.

Silver reaches into his butt pack. "The lights are what're killing our batteries." He keeps his eyes on the portal and pulls out a SAT phone, extending the antenna.

"Who you calling?" comes from Mangler. "Ghostbusters?"

"Want me to do it?" Nguyen asks.

After a moment, Silver looks up from the phone. "Be my guest," he says, handing over the dead hunk of plastic. "It's dead too."

Terp, having watched the beast, having felt the elation of its control, seen the new lights and the Americans squawking, addresses the team with uncanny volume. "What is all happening?"

"The devil," Hutch blurts, putting Silver half-back into reality when he peels away and posts himself in front of a window out in the hall.

"We don't know." Nguyen hands the phone back to Silver, locking eyes right as the light changes.

The green light, like the beast had done, is fading. It starts as a shimmer, brightening hot for an instant then cooling before crackling and gone. In blackness they all stare at one another, unable yet to remember the night vision resting atop their helmets. Nguyen is the one who says it: "Either it wasn't real or it went back, somewhere."

"What was?" Hutch says.

Silver looks at their Iraqi. "The monster," he says. "Terp." He slaps the page against the man's chest. "Can you read what you did for us again, one more time?"

12.

13 0141C SEP 05

They all leave the room, filing out into the hall. Nguyen moves down to the far window while the rest join Hutch. Mangler and Silver tug on Terp as he squirms free, placing himself behind Hutch as he begins to look down at the page.

Determined to bring back proof, even if it had to be developed later back in the damn States, Silver had pulled out his disposable camera he'd brought along; ready to capture a photo of Terp's next dragon.

As if called forth by the Iraqi's Arabic, the camera explodes in Silver's hand.

"Shit!" Mangler yells, flying to the floor.

AK rounds are peppering the front of the house. Some are making their way inside, like the one that just miraculously spared Silver his fingers. It is an instant, but enough to where naked eyes lock onto muzzle flashes; igniting from the roofs and windows of the nearby homes. Hugging the floor, protected by magicked brick, the Marines prepare.

Cracks against the side of the house pull Silver's eyes from the floor. Through the open doorway behind them, he sees the shards of the window he'd blasted break and shatter. "They're shooting at us!" he yells. "From out in the fields!" Rounds from a bigger gun tear through the front wall. "Everyone on the roof!" Silver doesn't just feel the heart-stopping terror as gunfire from two different directions begins ripping the walls to shreds. As he runs to the rear, Silver curses his sudden, irredeemable stupidity. They'd unleashed hellfire, and now all who'd best known nothing of their return were in positions to destroy them.

"Where's Nguyen?" Hutch yells. Mangler is halfway up the stairs. Silver flings the interpreter against its steps, following Hutch as the two run back.

Pieces of brick and plaster fill the air and scatter along the floor as Silver crawls back out into the hall. Nguyen is still—the window he lays under chipping away with every new bullet. "Oh, god," Silver gasps.

He grabs Hutch's leg, the force of the man's charge pulling him nearly to his feet before dragging Hutch, flailing and cursing, back behind the protection of the corner. Somewhere outside, the wall-slicing power of an RPK machine gun had nearly obliterated the door. Hutch squirms and screams, but Silver will not let him go. "He's in there, he's in there," means nothing until, by managing to wrench his rifle under Silver's arm, Hutch breaks free to round the bend and jump and spin back into Silver's grasp.

"He's hit!"

"Hutch, get the fuck upstairs—*now!*"

Hutch stares, unblinking. There is a moment; the disintegrating walls flutter their spore into the twilight between them, onto their shoulders, and then Hutch is gone.

There was no mistaking the dark pool growing around Nguyen. He lays on his stomach, his head facing away. Silver fights free of every better instinct, turning back to the staircase. As he does, seeping out from that one peculiar room, the green returns.

Alone, Silver runs up the stairs. Mangler's SAW is now engaged, each lunge up the stairs carrying Silver that much closer to its full spit. He hurdles over Terp and joins Hutch behind one of the parapets. These low walls are the roof's key feature, giving more than the advantage of height. What concealment they have may be little, ducking and scurrying to new places to rise up and show the flash of their own muzzles. But they are alive, and they are zeroing in with bursts upon their enemy. Mangler takes on the row of homes, Hutch and Silver the shooters out in the shadows.

Mangler knows when he hears it. Silver, too. A deeper firing suddenly gone, the Mangler had taken out the RPK. Their MBITRs still not working, Silver shouts over.

"No!" Mangler yells back. "Nobody! Where the fuck's Nguyen?"

No enemy had made their charge, not from the houses or out from in the fields. Silver fears most what will happen if the farmhouse is infiltrated. Grenades bounced down the stairs may make for easy work, but they—it hit Silver fully, right then and there—they were down now to three.

Spreading out in the shape of an L, countering the same shape their foe had caught them in, what remained of Stygian 2-3 soon gains fire superiority. AKs grow reluctant as those who dared fire at the Marines are put down. With every changing magazine Silver feels their odds improve. With the enemy's heavy gun finished, the parapets guard them from the chaotic attempts by their enemy to regain a losing ambush. The roof was an impenetrable sanctuary.

Then they hear the mortar.

From behind the row, a hollow *flume* rings out. Not a man, Iraqi or otherwise, shoots their weapon. The whole battle listens before an explosion tears a crater out of the earth, just below the nose of Mangler's SAW. He looks over the parapet, seeing that the next one, if adjusted, would be landing in their laps. "Mortars!" he screams, making a full sprint toward the mouth of the stairs.

Silver yanks Terp, who'd been reduced to a crying ball. "Summon it—you pussy. Summon it now!"

"One more mortar," Hutch pants behind him, "we're done."

"Summon it again," Silver demands, waving the others to pass him and get back inside. They remain, listening now for the next *flume*. "Now, Terp!"

His hand shakes, but Terp reads. Silver's eyes bear down on the exact line as the Iraqi tracks it with his finger. Through tears the beast wings above them, already obeying Silver's commands set upon Terp. "What now?" the interpreter cries.

Silver hears the enemy out there; frantic and enraged. "Send it over. Take out that mortar team."

Terp closes his eyes and utters the words. It starts flying, loping and low.

"You gotta be shittin' me." Hutch runs to the front. Silver and Mangler are right behind him, all now below the parapet's lip as desperate gunfire peppers the front of the house. Then the gunfire stops.

"It's gonna work," Silver whispers.

His team now spread out, their hearts cheer as men begin screaming in Arabic below. Wings flap, kicking up sand. Now it is their turn—the shitheads—to fire in vain as a beast destined to devour them closes in.

But the monster screeches—a ripping whistle that rolls in every direction. Wheeling its great wings, the monster reels back, climbing with each whoop higher and higher, away from the Marine's enemy.

"Look," Silver says, furiously shaking his head until believing what his eyes see. Something else is flying, released from the houses and speeding towards *their* beast. They all see it now; much smaller than their winged weapon, this vague shape of a man, darkened with bat-like wings and a long, whipping tail, this creature, summoned by the enemy, rockets up and latches onto the beast's exposed belly.

"What the hell did they summon?" Silver grills Terp, shakes him, curses him until the pleading man can show no more than confusion.

"It's comin' back down!" Hutch yells.

Mangler shoulders his SAW. *Their* monster had fled toward the moon. This monster, appearing ever larger now, had turned is leathery glide, and is heading toward them. Every weapon fires.

Every man's throat tightens, and the vile demonic object soars through their offensive to pummel Terp into a screaming pile.

Wet heat sprays Silver. Through the rifle fire, a large bone snaps like wood. The creature rips and mangles, ending the 'terp, keeping silent as it scrambles down the staircase and then disappears. Talons scraping against the floor below are outdone by renewed gunfire. But not from the Marines. Crazed by their summoned demon, the mortar team had grabbed their rifles. Under the cover fire from distant windows, shadows now run toward the farmhouse.

2-3 forms a line behind the parapet. No man talks. No man fears. Adrenaline had dumped and re-dumped and coursed to where fear and courage and murder had all become one. They stand, wide-legged, trained through their sights to drop each one of these moon-lit madmen.

Drop them they do. Bounding fools were no match for rifle's running hot and dry, low on spare mags and fatally on target. Directly below, in spite of the war, Silver hears wings flap then fold, he *feels* horns atop a black head ram the front door to splinters. Its wings now spreading, its talons gripping the limp, lifeless body of Nguyen, the demon flies off.

"Help him!" Hutch screams, spiraling to delirium as his rifle suddenly jams.

"Oh my god." Silver can hardly breathe.

Mangler shoots at the thing until it is but a speck amongst stars and his barrel burns red.

Those out in the field had maintained their positions, saving not a bullet. This enemy base of fire made the roof suicide. The next AK blast sends out a close one; rattling Silver's helmet with a glancing blow.

"He's takin' 'im! He's takin' 'im!" Hutch screeches, clearing his barrel and blasting at the sky. Hutch's chaos is drowned out by an eruption of AKs. The cacophony puts fear back in Silver's heart. It sounds like more gunmen have arrived. Reinforcements to send him and his team to oblivion. Out in the field, muzzles flash and they aim, then all ends, save for—

Silver strains his naked vision. He sees it, too clear to be real. Two green orbs are glowing, out there, no different than the lit wide eyes of some alien animal. "Jesus," he says. "There's something else, something else out there."

And the enemy gunfire is gone.

Sergeant Miller floats above the men who he just killed, his two AKs still smoking from their barrels. He pulls back and flies higher, watching from above as the Marines leave the roof, the farmhouse where Ortiz had died, and watches the three make entry into the row, listening as they kill in each and every room that demands it. He then flies away, his eyes flashing their radiant green.

13.

14 0720C SEP 05

"It's fantastic we have over a dozen bodies now to sort through—but, in case you haven't noticed, Corporal Silver, a pretty darn important one's missing." The major had been speaking this way ever since the three shuffled across the cement of the company office.

Not only the company commander and Lieutenant Ashton, but seated at the table now is the battalion commander and even the towering full-bird in charge of the entire regimental combat team. The colonel adds to the embarrassment; "I believe an interpreter is gone, too."

"Corporal Silver," the major leans forward. "*Where* is Nguyen? What we scraped up of your damn 'terp looks like ten mortars took him out, but I ask you again, what happened to your man?"

Silver sits in the center of the room on a wooden stool. "They," he fights the urge to look back at Mangler and Hutch. "They took him, sir."

"How? And where? Where were you?"

"On the roof."

"And they just rolled up in a truck," the major snarls. "And took him? Took Corporal Nguyen?" The only rolling done had been the evacuation. Silver attempted to call right after the fighters out in the field had mysteriously stopped firing. More mysterious yet, that bloodbath had resulted in three Muj fighters out there having apparently killed one another. Such bizarre luck had prompted Silver to pull out his SAT phone. It hadn't worked, and the enemy were still taking potshots from the row.

The last stand from inside beckoned the team's full aggression. Descending the stairs and using the rear door, 2-3 punched through the spaces, entering, shooting, destroying, and finally, once lathered in the fluids and grime of all-out war, were able to catch a break. Green back in the farmhouse had ceased to glow, and Silver soon had Higher scrambling to send out their convoy.

"I guess we can't crush your nuts for, *again*, not calling in." The major mixes his pageant with genuine, irked confusion. "Your man—and now a damn radio—is in the hands of the enemy."

Silver is on his feet. "Here," he unfolds the strange page he'd found the first night. "Here. All this writing, it means something. Terp read a line, I can show you which one. It makes a dragon appear. It didn't hurt us. In fact, the interpreter, before he was killed...by another thing, he was able to sort of control it." He looks at Lieutenant Ashton. The LT's eyes have gone from crisp to contempt. "Then the other thing, which also flew, it flew at us, killed our interpreter—it wasn't a mortar that got 'em—and then..." He feels the onset of tears, tears for too many things, though he fights them all back. "Then it flew off with Nguyen—Corporal Nguyen. He was already dead, sir."

Stern-faced, unmoved officers now stare. "Marine," the battalion commander clicks the back button of his pen, strafing Silver and the two behind him with his good eye. "I'm not going to ask your boys what happened. This is your team. You're going to go, right after chow, to medical and have a long talk with Doc."

"And while you're proving that you are or are not completely nuts," Lieutenant Ashton can no longer restrain his froth. "I'll deal with Nguyen. It'll be a search I can assure you, you will not be a part of. We may have you three help with gate guard the rest of the deployment while we mitigate new radio encryptions from here to goddamn Tikrit."

The major scowls at Silver. "Anything else?"

Silver joins Mangler and Hutch as they're ushered out. "The dead the convoy brought back, sir." He hadn't checked. He didn't need to. "They're all going to have that tattoo."

That evening the air cooled, beginning the creeping solace of shadows and ending a pallid day full of concerned brothers and steel-eyed glares. A tasteless lunch and a worse dinner later, Silver slogged from one fitful state to the next, ending at Greene's consoling Quadcon.

Folded in his pocket is the page Terp had read. Silver is determined. This may very well be insanity, but learning more may be the best effort being made to find the corpse of his radio operator.

He waved off Greene's offer. A shot of liquor, he feared, would rip free the stitching that was barely keeping him together. He continues, "We're non-op now. Stuck inside until further notice."

"I heard," Greene says, his eyes revealing he knows more.

"They're looking for him now. *Nguyen*." Silver sinks into abject humiliation. Hours ago, he'd had to watch as grunt units rolled out. He had tried to look down at the gravel when every other team in his battalion had marched past, all on their way to join a cause he knew was utterly futile. They wouldn't find Nguyen. He knew he'd also come to vent. It took only one soft question before Silver confides in Greene. He tells him the whole story.

"I told Doc I'd made everything up," he feels his throat become a knot. "I said seeing Nguyen die shook me up so bad that I didn't know why I said what I did." Greene watches the way a man does when torn by what to believe. Silver doesn't notice. He looks around blankly at the fans and the radios. "I stuck to the whole green-light thing, though," he says. "That's the one thing LT thinks isn't bullshit. I'm done. I wrapped up the *interview* saying maybe the Muj is dealing in hazardous waste, trying to make dirty bombs or something. Maybe it effected my vision."

"…But there wasn't hazardous waste."

"We ran into that new cell, man. I shit you not, there were monsters flying around."

Greene stares at him. He puts his head in his hands, rubbing his face like he's trying to wash something off before consulting a fresh report. He turns back to Silver. "We caught wind that the Iraqis saw something too last night."

"What?" Silver's eyes grow hard.

"Flyers."

"Flyers? How many?"

"Counter battery radar said they picked up two. They went different ways, and were small, but if CBR picked 'em up it means there was metal."

Silver knows one had to have been that thing flying off with Nguyen. *What was the other one?* Nguyen had all his gear, but the dragon had no metal. He scratches his head and laughs, pitifully. "They're gonna find nothing. That 'terp said something about there being portals."

"They're still searching for those guys," Greene says. "The ones that left the hospital. Now they're sayin' they all left together. Doesn't make sense. One was fuckin' crippled."

Silver looks over at a map on the wall. "Shit's gone insane. Where did CBR see everything?" Greene spins around and checks his computer screen. When he reads off the coordinates, Silver is in front of the map, tracing the latitude until the tip of his finger points at: "It's the farmhouse."

"Whatever those two things were, they got high and took off in a hurry." Greene spins back around. "Man, you still got that page on you? That weird big one?"

Greene was good, but reading minds? Though it came with great caution, Silver knows speaking its dreaded contents would whirl into action shit right out of a story book. He has half a mind to let Greene do just that. Higher would be left with a quivering lip when a few dragons flapped and perched in the motor pool.

Silver reaches into his pocket then stops. "You believe what I'm telling you, right?"

"I don't know. You're not exactly the type to lie, man. But..." Greene seems to invert. "*But*, what's going on right now, I guess I don't know what to believe."

Silver hands Greene the page. "Can you figure out what this is?"

"Man, I don't want nuthin' to do with this evil shit—I just wanted to loo—"

"Then promise me, Greene. Promise me right now. Translate, but don't you read any of this shit out loud." Silver grabs the loaded Listerine bottle. "At least not yet."

Greene licks his lips, tempted, but he also sees the careful, calculated fear in the eyes of the warrior before him. He reads aloud a solitary word. Silver seizes him by the neck so hard, so fast he can't feel the fingernails digging in. "Okay—*aghk*" Greene breaks loose. "Okay, man—Jesus. I won't...sit down."

Silver pours a shot. "Just see what you can make of all that." He swallows then pours another, sliding this one over to Greene.

One incantation had given them a cowardly, winged giant. But, having triumphed a hard pragmatism at last over the awes of his fantasy, the incantation had honestly bore them little else. Silver figured the lethal being that had taken Nguyen had been summoned in a similar fashion, by the members of that new cell, wisped off pages from the same dark source as the paper Greene now held. It would be fully night soon, and then, under the grace of shadow and stars, he would permit an experiment or two.

14.

14 2206C SEP 05

The night had turned bitingly cold. A glitch somewhere was cutting the camp's power, calling generators into action, brightening and darkening the whole lot in a succession of sluggish, orange blinks.

"What the hell we doin'?" Greene asks again as they shuffle out.

He'd repeated the question enough to heighten Silver's discomfort. Silver knows what they are about to do is nothing short of reckless, but a desperation had steadily crept in, resting there until, perhaps, something could be done.

Silver had taken a headlamp off Greene's desk. Now wearing it, he clicks its blue light. In an empty square of gravel, they stand and scan the lifelessness of the MEK. Silver unfolds the page again. "Our interpreter read *this* line. I want you to read it?"

"Why? So I can end up like him?"

Somewhere between the fifth shot and the sixth, the weight of Nguyen's death pinned Silver to his chair. Yes, Ellers had been killed too. But there was no comparison. Seeing men ripped from the prime of life left many service members in a bizarre state of contemplation. An IED that liquefies a man's body—*Where* is *he?* a witnessing survivor may soon wonder.

Mirthful chats about what college they'll all go to once out, stopped from ever being able to become true by the aim of a gun— *What is then left of this man?*

Ellers had been hit, but his remains were on a plane, bound for some state and a funeral. Nguyen's death and the subsequent missing body had become a waking nightmare.

"I don't know, Greene." Silver tries to hand Greene the page, but this time Greene isn't accepting it. Silver points to the line Terp had read, cringing at the sudden thought of what might be happening to Nguyen's body. "This may be the only way we get him back."

The past hour or so, what was usually a spirited drinking session had been replaced by an ominous bout devoid of all chit-chat. Certainly, Greene understood. The loss. The fighting. Hell, to a Spartan type, being put on non-operational was like being cast out of Heaven. But still, Silver's behavior was more unusual than even such extreme circumstances would normally allow. The whole of Greene's intrigue, his tipsiness, his skepticism, all then came up with the tone in which he asked: "How?"

"I need you to summon the same thing our 'terp did," Silver says. "Out there."

Greene's frayed laugh steams from his mouth. "Dude, do you have any idea how you sound right now? You may need to...so what, I just pick up and start reading?"

Silver knows that he had done well, out there. Petty worries melt as he ponders the phenomena. More than occurred—he'd created the phenomena, or at least had played part. "I know the line," he says, his breath matching Greene's. "I just need you to read it."

"And you aren't gonna go for my neck?"

Silver blues the page with his headlamp. He points to a string of words.

Greene takes his hands out of his pockets but he doesn't take the page. He looks up. "So when this shit doesn't work, do I or do I not report your ass to the nearest wizard?"

"When you read it, I promise you, *you're* gonna wanna see the nearest wizard. Just try not to scream."

Greene shakes his head and bears down on the words.

"Wait—" Silver says, jumping Greene out of his skin.

"What now, man?" Greene twitches, looking over his shoulder.

"Do you see anything about, I don't know, a dispel magic kinda thing?"

Greene reads the words.

"Oh, fuck!" Greene yells, and Silver does not move as Greene falls down onto the gravel.

Silver stands above Greene. And behind Silver, as real as the page Greene had refused to touch, is the great beast he then gazes up at before looking back down to Greene.

"*Shhhhh.*" Silver presses his finger not against his own, but the trembling lips of his new reader.

Greene crawls backwards until his head hits the side of the Quadcon.

Silver smiles, oddly.

Giant wings begin to unfold.

"Looks like you didn't read the whole thing," Silver says, turning from his upward inventory back to Greene. "Terp had it mimicking him. Is there another part?" Silver bends forward, holding the page and its words.

"Uh—yeah, yeah. Right there." Greene points to a spot near the incantation. "Says…belong to me."

"Read it."

When he does, the giant follows suit, sending the weight of its collapse into the ground and up Silver's legs. "Oh my god," is all Greene can say. He says it more than once.

The tiny earthquake subsiding, a sudden pang of fear strikes Silver.

"Quick," Silver says. "There's some kind of dispel magic—some kinda time limit. Get him out of here."

Greene scrutinizes the page, swelling and speaking another string. When the beast vanishes, Silver pulls Greene off the gravel and out of his dumbfoundedness, both running and giggling back into the Quadcon.

Laughter, yes, for it was impossible not to. Silver figures his old drill instructors would salivate if they somehow learned his fear of getting caught is what drove him to flee back into the concealment of Greene's workspace—rather than the sane, mortal concerns over the appearance of what Greene now laughed repeatedly, he could hardly believe.

For Silver, their shared lunatic giddiness is due to an exhilaration of control, the now-knowing that he could harness an obscure but very real, very callable power. For Greene it was the sudden connecting of many dots.

"So that tattoo," Greene says, out of breath and shutting the door. "The one smack dab centered on this page here. It's all connected."

"I know, but how?"

Greene disappears in the back and remerges with a book. Greene is flipping through pages then comes under a light and stops. "I cannot freakin' believe it. It can't be."

"What? What, man?"

Greene says nothing. His eyes have locked onto a page that Silver can't see. "I don't know how this is all happening." Greene flings his eyes off the gloss. "It's like Lovecraft knew."

"Knew *what*?"

Greene seems to hesitate, then slowly closes the book. "Here," he says, tossing it to Silver.

Silver looks at the cover, recognizing it immediately as what Greene had referred to a few days prior. "*The Complete Illustrated Guide to H.P. Lovecraft,*" Silver reads the title. "And?"

"Go to *S*," Greene says. "*Shantak.*"

Silver opens the thick hardcover. Flipping as Greene did through an encyclopedia of monsters until coming to a page with an archaic, tentacle-wrapped capital *S*. Silver knows what Greene is thinking. "Scathach," Silver reads out, flipping as he goes. "Serpent Man, Sfatlicllp, Shabbith-Ka, Shaggai, Shan..."

"Yeah," Greene says, placing his hands on his desk, staring at Silver. "You see what I mean?"

Silver has no words. He can only equal the intensity, looking down at the exact creature. Terp had summoned the giant Shantak, the giant with its "bat-like wings" and "horse-like head." Now Greene had called forth a Shantak, too. Sending it back to...to—

"They come from the Dreamlands."

"How?" Silver says. "How the hell is this all connected?"

Greene comes alive and moves around the desk, grabbing the book. "You said that the other thing looked kinda human, right? Like a demon? Had wings and a tail. And you said the Shantak was scared of it, right? Bam—" He flips to *N*. "Nightgaunt," Greene says, almost proudly. "That it?"

On this new page, cast in the light of a laminated moon, perched on the roof of a church stood the spread-winged terror.

"Greene," Silver says. "Teach me everything."

15.

`14 2347C SEP 05`

Greene empties his bottle into the waiting cap. Seated now, he ignores a handset busy crackling on his desk; pulling Arabic chants up its chord into the small space that is now otherwise silent.

It had been exhausting, explaining the mythos to Silver: who Lovecraft was, and, how after he'd died, more than one book-crazed zealot had stood fast that the gentle recluse hadn't penned peculiar nightmarish fiction, but had bent his ear to the cosmos, transcribing things and beings and gods who truly were. Who *are*. If it was reality—being able to bring into flesh the creatures he'd put on paper close to a hundred years ago—then those zealots had been right all along.

Whatever disbelief Silver may have still clung to fled forever when Greene found *Thunn'ha* amongst the text of the confiscated page. Reading the incantation that it was incased in, Greene pointed then to the large humanoid frogs, patrolling a day lit fen in their now guidebook. Silver had watched as a mummified version of such appeared on the floor between them, long dead and motionless— even when Greene sent the corpse back in a flittering whirl.

A host of beings lay in wait on the other side. An ancient page struck true Lovecraft's malign world. Greene knew, dabbling in such affairs was incredibly dangerous. No such pleas however stopped Silver from dragging him outside, one more time, this fevered experiment driven by an excited command he summon a Shantak and order it to "Find Nguyen." When the beast reappeared, its languid nature and unflapped wings sent Silver back inside. Cries from somewhere nearby hastened Greene's ending of the spell. The last thing he wanted was firmly agreed upon. Spectacular though it was, what deep magic they were wading through was best kept under wraps until having learned more.

Silver left with a co-sworn allegiance: they'd keep their discovery a secret. If summoning the Lovecraftian was the only insanity to fall in Greene's lap, perhaps he would have raced to rejoin Silver in his trailer. But a series of recent events were unfolding and were starting to tie together. Greene had another concern.

Ever since the first reports started coming in about a child leader, many times when he was on his radios, Greene got jammed by some strange chant that soon dissolved his comms to static.

In Silver's linear determination, he hadn't noticed the generators lining the outside of the Quadcon. Connected to the necessary ports, Greene's batteries now had their reinforcements. Greene had just pulled all the recoil cords. Liquor-wanting Motor T guys could go without the machines. Greene had started them one by one, moving back into his dark space and strapping in for another war. One generator had prolonged his ability to listen, three, rumbling and growling, may be able to bat back whatever was assailing his main radio.

Greene downs what he hopes is his last shot of the evening. That damn chanting already in full sway, he puts the handset to his ear.

The imam bellows. All four lanterns pulse in the stone room's corners, brightening and dimming in accordance with his call.

Of all the bodies now littering the streets and bloating in the calm waters of shallow canals, one had been plucked out from the wondrous carnage. On the imam's table, a corpse lay concealed under a clean white sheet. Sitting on the table, resting her hand on the corpse's covered knee, the child swings her feet, watching through her black sunglasses as the imam struggles at the window.

The old but not grey imam is aware of the efforts being made to listen in on the Sect. Caught and tortured jihadists had revealed to them the American's machined power. The Sect was bestowed abilities older and stronger than the likes of radar or radio wave. *But* it was undoubtedly the charge of their dutiful leader to combat the invader's irksome, constant meddling.

In the small secret room in the back of an otherwise ordinary mosque, the imam spreads his footing wider on the bald, polished floor. His pupil-dark thobe and shemagh flutter toward the night; a chilled September blackness sucking his words out into the open air. In his mind's eye, he can see Sergeant Greene, miles away; running outside to check his generators. The war—the ethereal war—is on now, smothering the distant Greene's receptions as the unholy man closes his eyes and concentrates, projecting his power.

The child watches him, paying no mind to the bugs that strut and preen along the table.

The imam spreads his arms. His fingers cringe as if about to surmount some unseeable, high-rising object. What his nemesis is doing he does not know, but he *feels*—feels by the acid in his ache and the sweat dripping off his brow that this time is coming the slow slip of defeat.

He opens his eyes, gulping in a breath which he suddenly expels. Greene's efforts, without knowing, crushingly wins. The imam is flung backwards, skidding across the floor, ending in a flailing heap at the foot of their symbol.

The child springs to her feet as something then flies through their window.

Eyes glowing, lips cracked and burned, Sergeant Miller calls upon deeply bruised arms to lift and point his weapons. The table's lone chair becomes splinters when the child sends it rocketing into the path of AK fire. Miller recovers from the knock, spraying holes into the skin-taught painting.

"One of you!?" Miller cries. "I am *not* one of you!"

The child is under the table, nimbler than a cat. The imam howls after a round tears through his shoulder.

Miller drops the AK in his right hand. No time for a mag change. Tossing the remaining rifle over to his dominant hand, he rises so fast and high his wind leaves him when his back slams against the ceiling. The imam is yelling at the child, for the child, extending forward a useless hand that will not stop Miller's next bullet.

Miller scans the room with his green eyes. Renewing his aim, he fires down at the table and the covered corpse laying on top of it. Shell casings fall, the wood between him and that evil little girl splits and thrums and splinters up and out, everywhere, as the child flies; coming eye-level.

Her gaze no different, the room lights lime as she bleeds from a bullet wound in her leg. What she utters Miller cannot hear, but what she does with her hands loosens Miller's hold on his only weapon.

She snarls.

Miller screams as grotesque pain electrifies his senses. Whatever hex has just deprived him of his rifle is but a start. Her arms now end not with cruel brown fingers, but with screaming mouths themselves. Before he can fly, before he can mount a desperate head-butt or spit in the bitch's leering face—the screaming mouths take hold, chewing with fangs and molars the bones in Miller's right hand.

The child laughs. The child, she ends her black unknowable words as Miller gapes at the bloody stump spurting before him.

"Meet oblivion," says the girl, too deep for a human throat. Floating backwards, her garments flap, dripping blood to the floor. Her hands now returning, shell casings rise to greet her next brewing spell.

Miller shoots forward, blindly, without hope, ramming into her ribs, toppling the rising imam and pummeling her little body against the wall. He screams as he rips free the glass of the nearest lantern. His hand seared, his blood pouring, he sticks his exposed wrist into the open flame. The imam is crawling towards an AK-47 now. The girl is recovering, wobbling on all fours. Miller shoots past, screaming, close-lining the imam as he flies back out the window.

16.

`15 0300C SEP 05`

Nguyen's eyes open. With cold hands he grips the white, bullet-mangled sheet that covers him and pulls it down to his waist.

A tan moon hangs over him. It leers, its long yellow teeth unable to hide the moon's joy.

Men shout oaths from every corner of the room. Then something else.

It isn't Arabic. It isn't English, but Nguyen's dead ears hear. "Tool of the crawling chaos," the moon says, *"rise."*

Through a dry throat, Nguyen whispers, "Where?"

The moon pulls back, becoming the bearded face of an old man. "You are in," the old but not grey man says, matching Nguyen's English and gazing up at the ceiling. "Merely an old, ordinary mosque."

The new injuries Nguyen had just suffered meant nothing, for unlife had yet to be breathed into the awakened.

Though in pain the imam still laughs, his eyes concentrating on the awakened tool's throat. That had been the only wound which mattered. The killing wound still there, a faithful round had sliced through the carotid artery and blasted to bits a now superfluous vertebrae. Save for radios and weapons, Nguyen sits up in the gear he'd died in.

Nguyen flops his head toward those who'd gathered. Grey, unblinking eyes watch with indifference as armed Iraqis kneel. Their fervent reverence would have chilled the blood of a living man, but this object of a dark miracle only sits on the wood of the shot-up table, watching as a little girl in black calls the Iraqis to their feet.

She is limping, favoring the leg not bandaged in a bloody dressing. No magic spins reality's golden light. Healing is merely of a biological power, no more divine than the coupling and birthing of extinct trillions. But death, death and its companions, destruction and perversion of mass, these were the domains in which their master worked.

The imam, this high covert agent, he laughs no longer. His wound also dressed, he grips his shoulder and grimaces, retreating his stare from his warriors onto what he and the child had called back.

The imam raises his good arm, letting his hand fall on Nguyen's shoulder. "You have a great task," the imam says. "One which you mustn't fail. The house in which you fought so bravely, do you know the man who used to pray within its walls? He is, now gone, unable to read the rites those of us more suitable sustain. He was a member. You, called back, brave soldier, you are now the most esteemed of our ranks. Not dead. Not alive. You shall go where we are yet unable."

"Where?"

The imam turns to his men. The child's recent appearance had swollen the Sect greater than he could have ever willed. Now, Allah-abandoning sons burned Qurans and itched with tattoos still scabbing.

"Inert in our rituals," he continues. "We obeyed the proclamation that he will return."

Nguyen feels nothing when the imam slaps his cheek.

"But only when sufficiently prompted—and that is why the arrival of, how you say, *coalition forces* is so...useful. The great sage, he too came from America, preparing the world for which fools took for a fool's tale. Mayhem, blood now spillable, this will invoke the prompting which I speak. Our master will come." Every eye follows the imam's pointed finger, ending at the girl, standing with arms crossed and a smirk on her face. "All the sooner with the arrival of our god's sudden lieutenant."

Sect fighters swarmed the place like hornets, standing guard in the busied mosque or eyes looking skyward from nearby rooftops. Serving the Sect just as well, once the gunfire no longer echoed, villagers had run barefoot and wailing, soon learning their ears had borne witness to an American attack on their beloved Islamic leader.

The imam's pain subverted a smile, soothing his outraged flock but encouraging them to gather arms all the same. The child had instructed him well. She, agent of cosmic malignancy itself, would help send soulless heaps to oblivion, but the constraints of flesh beckoned due course.

Nguyen's dead eyes reflect back the flicker of lanterns and the departure of the Sect's frontline as they march down the stairs to join their brethren out in the night. The child limps to a corner so that Nguyen cannot see. She emerges with a wrapped bundle. The imam plants himself in front of Nguyen, caressing the hole in his neck, eyeing their assassin.

"There is a man you must kill," the imam says.

"Where?" he groans, biting down so hard teeth crack.

"In the place they call the Camp Fallujah. The MEK." Nguyen's state allows the imam to reveal his own embarrassment. "He beat me—the man who listens," he says, regaining his composure. "He has ways of, of disrupting our cause." Greene's odd new powers and the sudden arrival of Miller was well connected. The imam's shielding spells had held impenetrable, until a few hours ago. It was as if Miller had been able to feel the shield, its weakening, and waited not a moment to strike. "Another of our troubles," the imam says, "just found us, here, having waited like a scorpion under a rock for my power to loosen—you see! You see my flesh, and her flesh, shot? A troublesome entry made by a flying nuisance, a magicked *coalition* member we will soon deal with."

The child sets the bundle on the table, unfurling at Nguyen's feet the rest of his gear. The imam grabs him by the blood and sand of his collar, fingering the night's bullet holes in his chest that meant nothing. "But you, you stand and you walk…you walk to your Camp Fallujah. Inside you kill the man, the one who listens."

In a brain strangled clean of living power, visions begin to appear in Nguyen's lethal, calibrating mind. Dead but not, living but not, screamingly delirious, Nguyen steps onto the floor. The child hands up his radios. The imam, his cold M4 rifle and his M9 Beretta.

17.

15 1012C SEP 05

"Hutch," Silver whispers in a way meant for no one else to hear, though everyone does.

The night had burned away, replacing the clear sky with a sun that analyzed everyone down on the MEK's gun range. Battalion always alternated which range days would be Stygian 2's and what hot, windless morning would be the right of a brother platoon. Stygian 3 had requalified the week prior, confirming battlesight zeroes and swapping out batteries in EOTechs for new ones that would carry them back out into the Zaidon.

Silver pulls Hutch by his arm, bringing him closer, trying not to give notice to all the eyes. "Shooting like shit is one thing, dude—but you just *flagged* someone."

Stating the obvious, Lance Corporal Hutchinson was having an inglorious morning; failing the first qual and then, retreating back to where Silver and Mangler both sat in confusion, pointed his M4 barrel right at a picket-line of thighs under the ammo awning.

By some miracle, a platoon full of trained observers hadn't seen Hutch's error. One grace note, sure, though Silver's morning was fairing no better. Word was the three veteran members of 2-3, it had been decided, would serve better augmented as gate guards. Lieutenant Ashton had made good on his threat. No less a demotion than stripped of their chest hair and plummeted to private, non-op had become the embarrassment of assisting MPs. In garrison, military police were the archnemeses of hard-partying, risk-loving recon men...who now would tell Silver and his men where to stand.

Hutch shrugs his arm free, saying nothing and scowling like a kid.

Silver takes a drink from a water bottle, refusing to acknowledge the creeping hangover that hadn't screwed up *his* ability to shoot. "If we wanna get back out there," he says to Hutch. "Off fuckin' gate guard, we gotta show our shit's dialed in."

Hutch sneers. "Silver, look, even if we did get put back on operational status, the team is down to three. We'll be sent to other teams." Hutch looks at Mangler then looks away. "I'm sorry Corporal, but our rep isn't coming back."

"With that attitude it sure as shit ain't." Silver bites his lip and ignores the snickers, soon convincing himself the range coach's call for the "Blind fuck" prevents him from putting Hutch right on his ass. "Go qual," he says, pointing at the miserable little stretch of sand Hutch will return to and try to hit the broad side of a barn.

The smell of gunpowder and rote commands of the range coach run berm to berm as Mangler and Silver can only shake their heads. Their usual dead-eye, in the prone, looking through sights that had already helped kill plenty, was again on his way to failure.

18.

15 2050C SEP 05

The crowded chow hall betrays the darkness waiting outside. Fluorescent lights hum. White gleams off the twin-tower posters; already being taken down and boxed up for next year. American flags still hang and flap in plastic unison, arching over the main entrance and ordaining the salad bar. Mangler and Silver are sitting side by side, eating from their trays, watching the news on a large flat-screen:

"At least twenty-six Iraqi police are dead," the FOX News blonde says into a camera overhead, *"Following two car bombs in Baghdad."*

Mangler looks at his tray. "You think they got any more—"

"Okay," Greene says, squeezing in, plopping down a tray full of—

"Dessert."

"I did a little more research," Greene says to Silver. "Your boy Mangler here, he up to speed?"

"He gets it," Silver takes a bite of his apple, staring up at the TV.

"All right, because y'all are gonna wanna hear this. And you're gonna see quick why we don't got time to be convincin' your main killer here that monsters are real."

Greene's sudden uplift in spirit takes Silver by surprise. A much needed one perhaps, for Hutch's sour shooting had mixed with rumors that he was rampantly telling all who'd listen that Silver was unfit to be a team leader. If Hutch had joined them for dinner it may have been Mangler peeling Silver off that piece of shit, rather than Filipino cooks peeling off the walls glossy reminders of why they were told they were there.

"What do you got for us, nerd?" Mangler says, scooping onto his tray a chunk of Greene's cobbler.

Silver smirks, giving them a sideways glance.

Greene reaches into his cargo pocket. "You motherfuckas aren't the only one with a *Rite in the Rain* notepad. Check it." Greene flips it open and starts reading. "All of Lovecraft's work, it involves this idea we are basically nothing. It's a *maligned universe. Cosmic indifference.* Why he stands out is because, before him, a scary story was just God and the Devil; the Devil usually winning."

The TV rages on: "*Elsewhere, three Shia pilgrims are shot dead by a passenger in a passing car traveling to Karbala.*"

Greene flips to another page. "With Lovecraft it was all different. A God's devil is a goddamn summer vacation. With him, the whole game changed. The world, the universe is against us—well, more like some of the universe is against us, the rest doesn't give a shit. But this is where it starts to matter. He used a lotta real world shit, too. In *The Key of Solomon*—"

"I've heard of that," Mangler says.

Greene closes his notepad. "You gonna tell me your goon ass knows *The Key of Solomon?*"

"*Heard of it.* Hutch talks about it. Some book his preacher back home doesn't like."

Greene opens his pad back up and looks over at Silver. "Well, well, recondo's got a library card. Well, your non-shootin' ass boy's preacher may know a thing or two. It was a *grimoire*," he'd pronounced it slow and irksome. "Written in the renaissance, but this ties to us, sittin' here in good old Iraq, because it was a bootleg of what Arab magicians were writing way before that."

Mangler snatches the pad. "Lemme see this—you actually wrote this shit down?"

"Silver...you gonna tell your boy to give me my shit back?"

"Boy," Silver says with devoutly no life. "Give him back his shit."

More than one table looks over when Mangler bursts out laughing. He leans in and whispers, "Greene, *Nigger Man?*"

Greene snatches back his pad. "It's a damn cat."

Above them, the television changes to a montage of fresh carnage. A voice excites: "*Two Iraqi police were also killed near Kirkuk and three civil servants die following an attack on the Ministry of Industry.*"

"You white boys are all crazy," Greene says. "But Lovecraft takes the cake, or at least I thought he did. Until I heard on the radio today who was in your damn farmhouse before y'all got there."

The change in Greene's tone stiffens Silver. "Who was in the farmhouse?" he says, looking at Mangler.

"Muj is saying somethin' big happened there on...and they even said the day." Consulting his notes, Greene sits straight. "The sixth— of this month. Not even a week ago."

"Who was in the farmhouse, Greene?"

"Silver—motherfucka—I'm gettin' to it. They were sayin' our boys rolled up and blue-on-blued some of our own, in that house. Turns out, who they lit up was a sniper team. One died. *And*, turns out also, the one who survived is one of those who went missin' out of Charlie Surgical. Turns out too, gossipin' nurses love whiskey, 'cause the missin' sniper's a guy named Paul Miller. A Sergeant. Now, follow me on this. Right after the farmhouse gets lit up—the one Sergeant Paul I'm-somehow-motherfuckin'-missin' Miller was hidin' in—reports start coming in about green lights."

"You are way too excited about this," Silver says.

"Yeah, well, shit gets deeper." Greene flips to a page he'd dog-eared. Fixing his glasses, he says, "Says in the," he stops, enunciating the entanglement one sound at a time: "The *Clav-icula Salomonis Regis*—if two summoning spells are read off in the same place, it opens a pathway. Now, I wouldn't think jack shit of this, if it weren't for the only translation of the *Necronomicon* available in Arabic. I don't know where, I don't know how, but the dudes who wrote it said the same thing."

A month ago, Silver would have teased Greene right out of the chow hall. But here he does not. He sits, broodingly, coming soon to a grim thought. "Back at the house, the 'terp summoned a Shantak once, then...then he did it again."

"Yeah," Greene says. "Two times."

"But the green lights," Mangler says, completely ignoring that the beast has a name, "weren't they getting reported before our 'terp did all that?"

Silver and Greene look at the other. At last Greene turns, "You right, dude."

"So," Silver says, relieved in some sense, "where does that leave us?"

Greene stares down at the table, rapping his knuckles. Mangler and Silver watch as their scholar twists and turns an object in his mind. He comes back. "Then it's gotta be Miller," Greene says. "A sniper—fuckin' up so bad a whole convoy lights him up?"

"Then he, this Miller, he summoned something?" Silver isn't sure if he asks or says it. "Twice?"

Greene is sure. "Or he did the second one, causin' an entire CAAT Team to come rollin' up on his ass. And who ever lived in that farmhouse must've done the first one." He nods down at his notes, keeping his eye on Silver. "Doesn't say there's an expiration date on this shit."

Mangler was an anomaly. Only a certain breed of warrior held a pragmatism so unyielding that their mind could accept new, insane truths, yet remain unrattled. Mangler sits up, grabbing his tray and heading for the trashcans. "Tell us how we're gonna fight this shit when I get back."

Greene watches as Mangler walks off. "Man," he says to Silver. "That's one dude you want on your side."

A smile grows inside of Silver. "And do we know how to *fight this shit*?" he says, his frown less severe. "Any useful monsters yet?"

"I hate to be the bearer of bad news, and maybe to you two it won't be a surprise, but from what I read the *duo-summoning* point becomes evil-shit ground zero. Lights and Shantaks are one thing, but it sounds like other things—shit with intelligence has emerged. Maybe out of the house. Maybe from somewhere else and are drawn to it, not sure."

Silver doesn't say anything, but his face does.

"That evil ass kid," Greene continues. "One report's now saying she's *a girl*. You tell me the last time a damn kid, let alone a female out here, put together a terror cell."

"It's more than that," Silver shakes his head. "These guys aren't terrorists."

"Yeah, man. I know that. I'm sayin'—"

"You think this all ties together with that tattoo?"

Greene's odd mirth now gone, he nods. Now it is time to deliver the bombshell; the piece of info a gone-down-the-rabbit-hole search seated in the MEK's internet center had just drummed up. "That tattoo. The Mark of Nyarlathotep. Yeah, I do."

"Nar-*what?*"

"Just the most evil dude on the planet. Well, plan*ets*."

Silver can't tell any longer if Greene is excited or terrified. "Well," Silver sighs, "I'm all ears."

"Yeah, you better be. The stories go he *does* come here, and through death, destruction and all that happy shit he hopes to, well, in a word, turn the world fuckin' crazy. Look, Silver, Shantaks are one thing. Nyarlathotep, he's—"

"And Iraqis," Silver scratches his chin, "have his symbol tattooed."

"The symbol of a god."

"He's a god?" Silver tries to read Greene's face. "And you think he's real?"

As the two marines stare at the other, a third now enters the chow hall. Covered in dust and his own, dried blood, he stands just beyond the threshold, his sun-scorched hands clutching a loaded M4.

First one, then two, then more and more personnel stop eating to make real with their eyes who is walking by them. A sanctimonious reminder, called out from someone; "You can't come in here all dirty like that!" is ignored. So are the rules for no loaded weapons, and not caking the mopped floor with the remnants of a day's long walk, prompted by dark dreams conjured up by new masters. Nguyen is white, and he is walking and he is now raising his M4. Nguyen walks up to Greene and points the barrel between his wide eyes.

Silver spins, grabbing the barrel as a round explodes through the TV above them. Before he can recognize the shooter, before he can inwardly quiver at the cold skin rot, festered in clumps on a face and neck half-boiled by the sun, Silver grabs the M4 with both hands and vies desperately for its possession.

They wrestle once again, kicking over chairs, sending marines and sailors screaming as bullets tear through floor and wall. The purest of tunnel vision gives way.

"Nguyen," Silver gasps, almost letting go. "How?"

Nguyen does not answer.

Silver's hand is seized by the rough flesh of Nguyen's own. The shark-like blankness of grey eyes do not look at Silver, but beyond him, recognizing no face, no name. Silver cries, pulling with all this might.

A blur appears, tackling Nguyen by his waist, sending the fight to the floor. "Stop—stop it, dude!" But Mangler then feels and knows what Silver's heart and mind is seeing—

"It's not him, dude!"

Greene saw it the clearest before a bullet narrowly missed his brain. Amid shrieks, the whole place has erupted, Mangler wrenches the rifle free. Mangler didn't think of kicking Nguyen, but he does, sending the toe of his boot against skull as Silver clings onto Nguyen like a spider.

Prompted by instinct, Mangler unloads the rifle, throwing it on their table as Silver climbs up Nguyen's body, trying in vain to grab his wrists. Nguyen's hands not only flail, they claw. Silver's face is their target before one ceases its slicing and grabs him by the throat.

With one arm Nguyen lifts Silver into the air. Straddling his choker, Silver plants his feet, grabbing Nguyen's wrist with both hands as he watches a lime lightning crackle in Nguyen's eye. Mangler does not see. His leap in the air brings his full weight onto Nguyen's chest, cracking the ribs that don't break.

Not out of pain does the tool of the Sect scream. Nguyen's back arches, his boots find no purchase. Pinned and pummeled under their combined weight, he strains his neck, as if listening. If a spoon would have fallen, Silver would swear he'd have watched it descend to the white mopped floor as slow and soft as down. Nguyen looks upon Greene; who, still frozen in his chair, shares Silver's realization; an assassin, a target, a terrible mission had been enacted, and was about to fail.

Nguyen cocks his head. "What?" growling sublime. He calls out again, this question, not to them, but to someone, someplace, somewhere other. He snaps his head—his face—his eyes, all onto Silver; grinning so wide and hard his chipped teeth burst. What Nguyen oaths Silver cannot tell, for in its horridness is heard the moaning and chanting of an Arabic voice on the wind.

Silver knows only that he is the new target, of something. He does not feel his own grip weaken, only the surge of strange power rattling through his veins. Silver slumps over, hitting the floor. Mangler sprawls out, trying desperately to make up for where Silver's body had been. The Mangler bears down with considerable weight, but not before Nguyen slips his pistol free, puts his Beretta in his own mouth, then pulls the trigger clean.

19.

`16 0117C SEP 05`

A bullet from an M4 screams, tearing through a Sect member's brain. The soldier on the other side of the rifle presses his hand against his thigh, hoping in a shadow of hope he'll find the moment to try and stop the bleeding.

His platoon, a young batch of grunts hailing from some Army fort, has been split in half. An IED hit the centerpiece of their seven-vehicle convoy, sending the HEMTT refueler up in flames. The three front Humvees wasted no time flinging dirt and pushed out of the ambush. The three in the rear ate the blast of the HEMTT's lacerated tank. Horror in the rear-views turned the front Humvees around, obliterating a fence and sending their axles creaking in desperate unison, screeching to a halt as the last man alive from the rear vehicles, stuck between appearing bongos and a burning Humvee, fell down into his own guts.

Now, soldiers position themselves between vehicular armor and behind their open doors. The Sect of the Faceless God is in full force. The child even chose to accompany them tonight. From a garage and a barber shop leaning against it, the Sect blasts their AKs. Another RPG flies over the Americans, turning a patch of black into a brief, violent white. Not four miles from the MEK, this rare nighttime attack had taken the platoon completely by surprise.

The soldier, the one with the leg wound, he watches from above his sights as severed Iraqi heads pop up from behind the garage's wall. He aims at one, regaining his crazed senses just long enough to lower his aim and empty his mag into the brick. Those on the other side, the ones holding and jostling the horrible skewers, succumb to his fire; returning their own from unseen holes that cost him his life.

Humvee tires are no match for the bullish force of 7.62. The rounds; angrier, fatter than the American 5.56, punch through thick rubber as they now do Kevlar and skull. The child tosses her skewer, mooshing her barefoot against the face of a local who wouldn't submit. The men firing from the barber's roof and from behind stacks of tires in the open garage, they stop. Their work is nearly done. Their sharpshooter had cleansed the dark world of these foreigners; scrambling for bulky weapons up in now useless turrets.

The child leaps, nimbly, onto and over the perimeter brick. The Sect of the Faceless God follows, turning their guns to put down a soldier crawling too close to a fallen weapon. The Sect, how they leer when she raises her arms to the moon. The next moment, from nowhere, from shadow blooms out full, thick, grey tentacles; spotted and tinged by red and gold. When flame finds the refueler's reservoir, all cover their faces, except for the tentacles' summoner. Fire dances in her sunglasses as the eyes glowing behind them watch on. Tentacles grapple with the ground, and with the bleeding limbs of the numerous dead.

"To the Faceless God!" the Sect cheers as one. "To the child!" Loose bands of jihadist scum would perhaps fire their weapons skyward. A sick, petty display. But these men, followers of the only true religion, crawl down from roofs and emerge from behind towers of planted rubber. They walk, they run and limp, all to kneel at the child's stoic hand.

A Humvee belches, covering the Sect in black smoke as it fishtails down the escape route the soldiers had first attempted. The tentacles, seated from someplace under the earth, slap against the driver's side. The Humvee grinds, pulling tight the appendages, making their slime gleam a long ribbon of the moon. A scream so shrill some of the Sect dives for cover—a hidden, badly wounded American charges. He runs toward the struggling Humvee. "Don't leave! Don't leave!" But a tentacle pulls him away, dragging the soldier down.

AK fire pops one of the back tires. The driver, who in his petrification had sought the refuge of his steering wheel, he finds the right gear and pushes the gas until his foot goes numb. That hideous coil holding the Humvee loosens. Thick, black rubber burns off the tires, printing on the hardball their forward gain until, at last, writhing, undulating, the tentacles release, sending the mangled Humvee screaming out into the fields.

20.

16 0817C SEP 05

"Why not?" the MP scoffs. All morning, Silver had retreated from one corner of the guard tower to the other. At about thirty feet high, the claustrophobic box provided little escape from his new colleague's needling.

"Because," he says, giving up, "I could go into DOD's rules on hygiene, human sexuality—"

"Ah," her eyes brighten, "there it is. The girls will wiggle their skirts and you big bad warrior boys won't be able to shoot your cool weapons."

From the rise of the sun, she'd been squawking his ear off about how women couldn't try out for recon. She'd rolled them all out; maxims of "Every Marine a rifleman," pleas that any who are willing should be given a shot, and, of course, smirked declarations that such progress would mar the good ol' boys club. Silver looks through their allotted binoculars. The barren plain outside the main gate was as he'd left it.

"No," he says. "Even if you were paragons of professionalism, team cohesion would take a hit." He is tempted to go into pelvic stress fractures and the ungodly weight of a fully-laden ruck, dropping the logic nuke and ending it there. But their ongoing talk, for all its canned and expected ribaldry, was at least a distraction. The MP's bun, if unfurled and behind closed doors, must've been a ponytail darker than wine. Her pear shape, when unburdened by cammies and clean armor, was still the tender body of a woman. Though not exactly pretty, a typical warmness he felt himself longing for rushed over him. She was all right.

"Team cohesion," she laughs. "Well, Corporal, looks like you boys already *took a hit*. Why the hell else would you be up here, with me?"

Silver puts down the binos and busies himself with some useless sheet attached to a clipboard. *God*, he thinks, *Will this ever end?* It softens the blow to know at least Mangler and Hutch are suffering the same, elsewhere at an equally obnoxious post. For all her chatter, the MP has said nothing Silver doesn't already know. Yes, there are now more reports streaming in about green lights, and yes, now there were freak strikes of phantom lightning, a phenomenon currently baffling the MEK's artillery meteorological team.

"You know I shot range high, right?"

"I did not," Silver says, feeling the convo of the hour clawing its way back to the surface.

"Why do you keep looking at your watch? Going out to snipe someone soon?"

Silver rattles off a joke that goes nowhere. At 0900 he has to trade this misery in for another. Lieutenant Ashton and the usual tribunal are demanding his, Mangler's, and Sergeant Greene's presence. Explaining the nightmare that had occurred in the chow hall where blood still clung to mops has him counting the minutes, not sure if his greater urge is to stay here or to run off screaming.

Far from done, the female MP shoulders her M16A2 rifle, looking through its iron sights, down its long barrel at a point somewhere on the ground. "You know," she goes. "The entire camp is talking about what happened last night. You guys are crazy—way worse than, god-forbid, a *wook* stinking up your ranks with her nasty tampon."

Silver tosses the clipboard. He bites his lip and seeks the refuge of the binos. He scans all that fronts the main gate. "You know," he says, feeling a headache coming on. "You know what, look up pelvic stress fractures, Sergeant."

Her *roger that* and *oorahs* go lost, drowned in the early morning as he aims what is left of his concentration out onto the road. It is calm cool weather at least. Fall mornings, when compelled to be charitable, were not unpleasant. Flaxen fields rolled, laid flat in places erect with power-line towers and where final stretches of civilization had insisted on houses in the sand. Green dots the dry earth. Shrubs and the far heads of palms do not move, as the brown speck Silver catches in the glass now does.

"You see this?"

"See what?" the MP says, losing her tone when Silver doesn't answer.

"A Humvee." Alone and limping, the vehicle is making its way up a dirt path his eyes now recognize as a derelict road.

"So?"

"It's not a part of any convoy—here." Silver hands her the binos, squinting now at the approaching Humvee. Soon no binos are needed. Alone—an oddity—odder still, no helmeted head is in the turret. The two can only look at the other as the Humvee comes to a rest outside their gate.

"The gate," she says.

Silver wastes no time. Down the ladder and lifting the boom, all machinery involved pries the great doors wide, and in crawls the carcass.

In a matter of minutes, after the MP got on her radio, after fresh haircuts stopped shoveling in chow, after Silver had hurriedly shut the gate; a crowd had gathered.

"Whose unit?" some officer declares as the crowd swells.

"Where's the rest?" a gunny asks Silver, receiving only a confused expression shared by all now ogling at what is left of a back tire and what had dried on the vehicle's paltry armor.

"Good golly," someone says. "What the Sam hell are they?"

Silver parts the swarm. Standing so close he can touch them, suction-like circles the size of dinner plates run along the entire driver's side.

"Son." A chaplain has joined the group, pulling out the driver. "Son, can you talk?"

Silver sees the guy's face. A soldier; kitted out for an operation that he knows ran into opposition beyond their power. The soldier has the eyes of Hutch, the eyes of Terp before he died.

The chaplain continues his plea, encouraging others softly to back away.

"Give 'em air."

"Get water."

In the end, the lone survivor only stares through them, breaking into sobs, petrified, and beyond talking.

21.

16 0902C SEP 05

If I have to see this room one more time, Silver thinks, fighting the pain in his temples, *I'm going to—*

The Stygian company office is bursting. Silver, Mangler, Hutch, and Greene all sit like criminals awaiting their executions while Lieutenant Ashton, alongside the company and battalion commanders, and other assorted brass, scowl and blink and continue to size them up from behind the table. The only new edition this morning is a pale, silent Charlie Surgical doctor, sitting in a far corner, burning a hole in his notes.

"I'll say it again, Marine." One of the grey-haired, dark-eyed officers points at Silver. "You and your boys haven't just seen the glory, but the gory of war. We all know it's been hard."

"Thank you, sir," Mangler, Hutch, Silver all seem to trip over the other to say, though not a one speaks a word with enthusiasm.

"Losing a man in combat is one thing," the officer affirms. "But this." Two things are no secret; Higher thinks Nguyen killed himself and Higher sure pities the shit out of the team over it now. It is true, in a form; Nguyen did jam that pistol up into his mouth and blow chunks of bone and brain across the chow hall floor. But Silver knew. So did Mangler. And so did goddamn Hutch—though not at dinner, he'd seen with a pair of perfectly good eyes the inconceivable first, real, only end to their radio operator.

Silver casts a glance his way. Little different than the surgeon— who, too, had been pulling Silver's eyes away the last few minutes from their firing squad. Hutch sat with his arms defiantly crossed with a dip in his mouth he must've been drinking, inspecting and re-inspecting the toe of his cleaned boot.

"Sir," Lieutenant Ashton speaks, looking down the table, across a landscape of notes, over to their senior man. "On behalf of all, I want to personally apologize. Our forces would've been better spent not looking for a man, well, one not wanting to be found, at the time at least."

Silver's head swims. His blood is coming to full boil. He can feel where this is all going. A sudden movement from Greene happens next. Silver may have turned to see what the other irate, too-informed among his throng is doing…but he deems himself unfit. Since Nguyen's hand had gripped his throat and those grey, hard eyes had pinned him as awful sounds rolled from that fattened tongue, a bedazzling series of headaches had quickly sought to crown Silver's misery. Every officer watches with noted disapproval as he swallows another Motrin.

"Gentlemen," Sergeant Greene stands, immediately stuffing back down his plea that Nyarlathotep be treated as real when every eye swings on him like an armored door.

Silver rubs his temples, but it's the Mangler who says it: "This is fuckin' bullshit."

The sum of Lieutenant Ashton's blood shunts to his face. Red and silent, every other officer's lips go thin and white as the head inquisitor, now, who through befogged, throbbing eyes Silver sees is a two-star general, looks amiable and concerned. "How so, son?"

Mangler and Silver bounce looks off one another, ending when they join Greene on their feet at parade rest. "Sir," Mangler says, earning the undivided attention of the surgeon. "Corporal Nguyen was shot and killed inside a farmhouse. We all saw."

Great weight and pain begins to lift from Silver as the surgeon rises. "Gentlemen," the man clears his throat. "As you know, I am not here to contest tactics. Only to provide a grieving family and a unit with a report all here well deserve."

The general looks at the three who are standing. Then he eyes Hutch; who remains seated, looking down. "Are you okay with hearing this, Marines?" the general says. "You don't have to."

Hutch looks at the surgeon. Eventually, everyone in the room does.

"Yes, sir," Silver says, fed by the hard nod given by Greene. "We'd like to hear the surgeon's findings."

A wartime surgeon; he is a man affixed to death and decay. Dutied to prevent both and often failing. Such a man should not have trembled at the thought of reading from harmless charts and pages about to be stamped forever as official. The man does tremble, though. He dithers, padding the floor with his boots, this way and that, taking in a breath so long and deep Silver is about to scream.

"The heart," the surgeon begins. "The brain, lining of the throat, all showed the early signs of decomp."

Silver is aware of six eyes. The surgeon's, nailed to his report without relent, his own, and how they are locked in undoubtedly now a skirmish with Lieutenant Ashton's. Ashton's slide off Silver as the surgeon pauses.

"Go on," the general says.

"In Corporal Jonathan Nguyen's abdomen were gases only found in bodies...post-mortem."

"Sir," Mangler speaks directly at Lieutenant Ashton. "We aren't lyin'. Nguyen was...was *dead*."

For a long while no one talks. The two-star seems content on tapping his pen, looking down on a report of his own. At last he raises his eyes and plants them on the awaiting surgeon. "Doc, if you want to file a report saying a Marine who committed suicide was already dead be my guest. But don't expect a lone goddamn soul to back it. Is it possible our severely dehydrated, severely delirious, severely shot-up by an AK-47 Marine may have incurred these symptoms as a result of hiding and marching through Iraq, days on end, and wounded?"

If Silver dared breathe, he'd explode. Mangler too, perhaps. Standing in their midst was the one man capable of confronting a baffled command, and now a growing, dangerous, desperate lie. Only in a war this stupid could something this big be ignored. Silver can't take his eyes off the surgeon.

Mangler had not seen Nguyen laying lifeless in a pool of his own blood. His loyalty came from belief in his team, and perhaps more importantly, his team leader. And for whatever doubts he may have harbored, they all saw a fiend fly off with a body that neither kicked or screamed. Hutch, however, had seen everything.

As if sensing the recollection, the general scans the entire row. "I think I want hear from the one Marine who isn't talking. Son," lifting Hutch's chin with a soothing tone no different than if he'd used his hands. "What say you?"

"Sir, our team left 'em, Corporal Jonathan Nguyen. He was alive, and I saw."

"You're a *fuckin'* liar!" Silver spirals, breaking the seal of his arms, replacing them behind his back an instant later.

"Well, sir," Ashton says, "I guess we know why our search produced jack. What we have here is a Marine." He scathes Silver up and down. "One who was shot up and abandoned. Then reappears and tries to kill his team leader because of it."

Silver knew Greene would take point, breaking every courtesy known to military protocol to now froth how Corporal Nguyen had been dead set on killing *him*. Silver confirms, as does Mangler, turning his ire away from Hutch to look each and every one of these deniers in their cold, self-righteous faces. But it's the surgeon who Silver shares his sagging gleam: one when two men know a going-nowhere truth.

"Silver, all you guys sit down," Ashton orders. "Doc," the lieutenant guides his tone. "Is it *possible* our marine's body is looking the way it is due to bad dehydration?"

"No, lieutenant. I'm sorry."

"Doc," The general grabs a new file, opening its flaps to feign a glance, "I'm reading your request. Naval Hospital Camp Lejeune? Good duty station. Family nearby? Maybe lookin' to hunt some deer?"

No one speaks. Silver can only shake his head until the two-star resumes. "We've got a grieving family, about to be grieving a whole lot worse. You gunk things up with your report as stands, I guarantee you you'll be plucking out thorns in Twentynine Palms until retirement. You got less than thirty days here and," consulting the whispers of the assorted brass, "Corporal Newjin's family has their whole lives to live with this. We clear?"

Silver watches, mouthing *no* as the surgeon nods at the floor. "Sir," the measly lifer eventually looks up and oaths. "The body is entirely normal, save for the nonfatal holes in his chest, legs and neck, and that fatal one at the top of his head. Suicide."

And, just like that, it is over. Nguyen's death would be ruled some PTSD dribble, and now more units were set to die. The surgeon is thanked and leaves dejected, refusing to look anywhere but the six inches in front of him.

"Corporal Silver," the battalion commander now says. "One of your own has said you left one of your own behind." Silver is pelted with threats of being written up and demoted until, at last, his dull acceptance of such prompts the conference to shift to more pressing affairs.

Gate guard was about to get a whole lot worse. That a deranged, dehydrated Marine was able to walk in unattended with no report to command or Charlie Surgical had the brass in a new uproar. Surely, it was somehow Silver's fault too. Nguyen still having his radios eased the blow, but security would be nailed up to an all-time high. Silver, Mangler and the traitorous Lance Corporal Hutchinson are assured they'll be spearheading the effort.

22.

`16 2150C SEP 05`

Mangler and Silver would have cornered Hutch if it hadn't been for Lieutenant Ashton, who, upon the meeting's acrimonious close, ordered Hutch to stay behind. Mangler stormed off to burn away his anger in the gym. Greene, too, left without a word, no doubt racing back to listen to his radios. It was Silver alone who put an ear to the company office door, discerning troubled mumbles until footsteps behind him sent him on his way.

The pre-dawn guard post had been the first factor. The second, this display of lies and cowardice. Combined with a growing headache, these sapped Silver of all strength as he'd slogged off to go wither in bed.

He was no fool. The headaches had started right after Nguyen. The pounding and throbbing and grains of glass grinding away in the four corners of his skull came in lieu of the most horrid of encounters. But, in some sense to his relief, when his eyelids were shut, shut for too long, screaming visions of Nguyen's "suicide" were not what passed before his eyes.

Growing in its intensity, each time becoming clearer, he sees the MEK. He is out amongst the trailers, wandering under the dawn. Holding their station above him are low clouds—too low, catching the pure focus of one who can only self-describe his observances as a waking, reoccurring dream. In them—*in the clouds*—there are things taking form, growing more distinct each time they appear in Silver's war-addled mind.

Now, approaching some untold hour of sleepless tossing and turning, the door of his trailer opens. "Missed you at chow," Greene says.

"Didn't feel much like being there."

Greene nods and looks around the room, saying nothing until he can't hold back any longer. "Look," he blurts, "this is gonna sound weird, but you got any idea where my Lovecraft books are?"

Silver chews on his last Motrin. The ceiling is white and sterile and as obnoxious as ever.

"I looked for 'em a minute ago," Greene takes a step closer. "They aren't in the Quadcon."

"Why the hell bother? You won't convince those pieces of shit of anything anyways."

"Bro, you might be missin' my point. Like, they're gone, as in somebody *took* them."

Silver sits up. Eyeing Greene bore a strange result. They'd just nearly missed death—by a man who'd known them, and them he. He'd been like a damn zombie. He'd died, been carted off by winged evil, patched up, somehow sent back here and Greene is worried about books?

"What are you getting at, Greene?"

"Not gettin' at nothing, man." Greene says. "I'm just sayin', I come back from chow and my footlocker's open. Shit got messed with."

"Your radios?"

"Nah, all good. Just the books."

In a normal, sane world, the theft of books overseas was as insignificant as all the other crap getting acquired from sun-up to sun-down. CDs, CD players, DVDs and every medium of jerk-worthy porn left momentarily unattended; all finding new owners as the ops grinded on and on.

But this is different. Silver realized that much. Maybe it was the unrelenting throb, grinding glass into his temples. A good excuse for a bad mood, but he knew.

Silver wrenches himself up, treating Greene to a show of wobbling like an old man.

"You good, dude?"

"Yeah," Silver sighs, touching his forehead.

"I'd have a headache too, I guess."

"Before we do anything, you're gonna have to forgive me but we're searching that shit heap of yours again."

"Whatever, bro. Let's go. You won't find 'em."

Silver points to the wall separating him from the remnants of his defunct team. "Let's grab Mangler too."

"Why?"

"Another set of eyes."

Greene rolls his. "All right, but I'm tellin' you."

"Yeah," Silver grabs his rifle. "I believe you."

Greene opens the door and follows Silver out onto the gravel. "He's a good dude," Green says. "Sure saved my ass." Like all MEK trailers, Mangler's and Hutch's room is no more than ten feet away. At the handle, Greene stops. "You gonna tell Mangler about the Shantak experiment?"

Silver motions for Greene to open the door. "Everything."

"Yeah, true. I guess he ain't playing company man like your boy Hutch either—yo, Mangler," Greene shouts, opening the door. "Put away the lube, homie."

The sound of that other name had tightened Silver. It occurred to him right then that he'd be inevitably confronting Hutch. For all the incessant pounding inside his skull, not one thump or shriek had come from the Mangler's and Hutch's room. Maybe the Mangler had done them all a favor and broke the redneck's skinny little neck.

"Nobody's home," Greene says as Silver steps into a Lysoled cavern. "Check the gym?"

Silver is looking at how Mangler packed all his gear. When the deployment began, Mangler, Hutch and Nguyen had all shared this room. With Ellers and Nguyen gone, this ten by ten was down to two. The room is an empty bunkbed in one corner and a disheveled bed topped only by its mattress and Hutch's sleeping bag. Near the wall locker where Hutch stows his gear, Mangler's sea bags and ruck are piled head-high.

Right then Mangler walks in. "Yeah, I'm moving in with you, Silver. Sorry, man."

Silver doesn't speak or return the slap on his shoulder. Silver is too busy. Not a moment before Mangler had stepped in, Silver had caught a glimpse of something sticking out between Hutch's mattress and the box spring. He walks over.

"What the fuck is that?" Mangler asks, more to Greene than to Silver, for in Greene's eyes it's apparent.

"Hutch stole these," Silver says, handing Greene back his books. "Yeah, man. Come on over. I don't blame you."

"Yo, what the fuck we gonna do about your boy?" Greene slaps two books together like cymbals. "You know he took these for a reason."

Mangler looks at the Lovecraft covers, doubly confused. "I've been avoiding that little shit all day. He's on guard post now."

"Probably a good thing." Greene wants to say something else but doesn't. He sees the discomfort on Silver's face; who is seeing the question boiling out of Mangler's.

"Greene," Silver says, leaving the trailer. "You catch Mangler up. I'm gonna go find that piece of shit."

They watch as Silver disappears in the twilight of the trailers. Halfway into his journey his headache turns him around. He makes it back to his and Mangler's room just in time to collapse, swearing to Mangler he'll confront Hutch in the morning.

23.

17 0009C SEP 05

Silver heads down the perilous trail of a fevered dream. Though its end obscure, its cause momentarily uncertain, in the velvet between awake and no longer, he can't help but sense Nguyen's touch.

Josh Silver is in his teenage bedroom. Palm fronds outside his window wave in the Florida sun, casting shadows that sway on his posters of Limp Bizkit and Korn. Guided by some strange sense, he follows an extension cord that he remembers starts from a plug behind his bed, snaking its way beneath that old blue rug, ending, he knew, in his closet where it fed secret UV lights for his pot plants.

He pulls the closet doors open. Where clothes and a BB gun and pot plants should all be there are only stars, burning, winking, staring as if eyes that had waited long to see him. Perhaps only one step further took him high off bare feet, high into the void where suns now sped past at a terrible speed.

Out here, truth was a lie and sane was that which had ruptured, dripping itself clean of all precepts. His flesh froze. His eyes boiled, clean out of earthly sockets. But still, he saw. Saw with new—saner eyes, eyes that glimpsed for a fleeting instant a snarling bloated planet.

He then found himself on his bed—his current bed—a Marine, back in Camp Fallujah.

Laying alone, unaware of the hour, he stumbles out to gaze up at a relentless sky. The trailer rows still bulk about him, only now their angles all seem wrong. Dead wrong. What was a door is now something, somehow other. What is now the sleekish side of a trailer weaves and reforms up to the belly of a rust-covered cloud. The morning sky, or perhaps a singular type of evening, swims in a wispy yellow and the bloodiest of red. In the clouds are faces. They call him. His name now rides on the wind. "Silll-verrrr," they call.

Never had Josh Silver heard the words, "Get out, man! Get out while you still can," screamed with such terror. Nguyen's voice carried the plea. Surviving death, carried in the arms of abomination—nothing, for the return of the real Nguyen was now the truest miracle. The voices, the ones without faces; they all knew, as Silver somehow knew, this was not a part of the plan.

Infecting a foe was better than nothing. Armed with the insanity given by those *out there*, properly afflicted, Silver's ruined mind would have torn in one instant the delicate fabric of 2-3 battling the Sect unbelievably alone. But Nguyen's icy touch had been too slow, his words, forced from dead lips uttered upon a man yet unwilling to crumble.

Somewhere a lone voice shrieks, higher than the rest, piercing the haze about him until, in some dim form of wisdom, Silver knows they are lying. He will not join them. Nguyen is now gone. No grace nor angel had pierced the clouds, Silver's ears, his whirl-gnarled mind. The voice, that of a small girl's, wails hatefully on. What affliction he is suffering he will not succumb to, not fully. This he knows, as only the captive of one's dream is able.

24.

17 0910C SEP 05

The chow hall is clean. Thundering with the arrival and departure of boots, the polished floor shines back the lights overhead. TVs squawk. More dead, but Silver doesn't care. With the headaches gone, he tears into his breakfast.

What he had dreamed, if it had been a dream, served him well. It was like in *The Lord of the Rings*; how Gandalf had said, by that instance with that crystal ball, they'd fortuned on seeing a glimpse of the enemy's plan. Long gone were his notions of real and unreal. Or so he'd thought. What is real is the evil afflicting Iraq fears him, and apparently fears Greene too.

As if summoned by his brain crackling the name, Greene sets his tray down, promptly ending Silver's good spirits.

"Hey," Greene says as if about to tell him he'd accidently slept with his sister. "I'm gonna take it you haven't heard. Some female MP sergeant is lighting up a storm on the radio because a one Lance Corporal *Hutch*inson is UA for their guard post."

Unauthorized Absence—the thought alone was all it took to sour Silver's eggs.

"Man, that's not all," Greene says, eyeing Silver with some concern. When he realizes Silver isn't going to respond he takes a breath and reports: "Sounds like the book thief has been spreading more rumors, too."

Now, Silver was aware of this. First thing this morning, after rising and stretching with the glory of no pounding head, he was accosted by the few in his battalion still willing to be seen near him.

Silver was apparently crazy and not fit for leadership. What Silver had yet to learn was Nguyen had been left in hostile territory, alive, evading like a magician all the way back to the MEK.

"And in a state of 'dehydrated rage'," Greene goes on, "he turned on *you*."

Silver is out the door before Greene can finish. Spinning Lieutenant Ashton's politically-charged proclamations into actual gossip was the final straw. Hutch had an ass-beating coming. As Silver parts the swarm of pointers and on-lookers, his fists become steel. There is a phenomenon in a combat zone so few understand. As Silver marches to the front gate, he feels its full force. Threats like roadside bombs and being bore through by hot flying metal did not make one immune to the frailties of the human ego. A thousand and one gunfights later, vicious lies, betrayal, thievery; all came to a simmering broil. The MP's insults bounce off Silver's back a moment after he confirms his shitbag isn't there. From the tower she yells. She spits, he is sure. He is bee-lining towards the damn gym. Not like a lie-spreading shitbag would be in a place like that. But he will slice through every damn sandbag, kick over every blood-stained mop if he has to.

Weights thump and clank. Every face swings their eyes from their mirrors or stupidly wipes away sweat; all to take in the maniac who'd barged in to glare in full cammies for a target that isn't there.

Mangler is at the free weights. "You good, dude?" he asks after a stare.

"Just find me that little fuck," is all Silver says, swinging around and knocking over two officers who receive no apology.

In the back of Silver's mind, he knows. He'd known the whole while; storming around the MEK, kicking at trash. In the back of his mind, the one recently bombarded with shit worse than pain, he knew. In some strange way he wanted to go to the places Hutch would not be. Now, as Silver approaches, as he watches the door to Hutch's trailer slowly shut, Silver knows there is no more delay.

"Who—" Silver draws it from the bottom of his gut, stamping his way inside. "The fuck do you think you ar—"

Silver is greeted only by the morning sun. The room's one window is open, swaying on its cheap fulcrum in the yellow-bright air.

"Out the window?" Silver yells, slipping into a laugh. "Chicken shit." Mangler and Silver have the day off—Hutch too, according to his blown-out thinking. Operate? Nope. Go outside the wire and be a Marine? Not anymore. The look on Hutch's face when he slinks back will be worth the wait.

Silver opens wide the wall locker, half-expecting to find Hutch hiding, and if not him, some irksome new discovery to hide from Lieutenant Ashton.

Weird how order makes a Marine hate another just that much less. By all accounts the wall locker is a simple, polished wooden rectangle; ordinary in all respects, thoughtfully divided in rows for ammo, tuna packs, dip, and a high papery of *Guns & Ammo.*

Silver makes no observances for the dust and sand riding the tread of his boots as he grabs one of the magazines and plops down on Hutch's bed. It was an exercise in control which he soon began, his blood pumping less furious as he arc-welded his eyes to an article going over the merits of Tenifer. These processes, he reads, are most commonly used on low-carbon steels. They are also, however, used on medium and even high-carbon steels. This may include spindles—

Boots crunch against the gravel outside. As they do again, and then again. Each time deflating perfectly Silver's pathetic attempt at distraction. But no one enters.

Why had Hutch turned on him? Silver sets down the magazine and stares up at the ceiling. Maybe he could reason with him. Hutch, after all, he'd been a formidable adversary. Out there, he'd blasted first. He'd listened. He'd ducked the same bullets Silver had. A formidable adversary indeed, to the same adversaries who killed Ellers, killed Nguyen, who were scheming maligned ploys at this very moment to take apart more life with means crueler than any firing squad.

A kink in Silver's neck had been tightening as the boots marched by. Silver uses the back of his head to move the sleeping bag. Doing no good, he sits up to ball it into a pillow. Once in his hands, he sees under the bag, unmistakably, there are streaks of red.

Blood stains the mattress, turning whiter areas pink where sweat may have earlier deluded. Most, covering a swath fitting the vague outline of a human torso, looks shockingly new. Silver looks for clots. There are none. He looks for some source or explanation, rendering little more than what a fist-fight looks like when wiped into a towel. He sees how it—what had to be Hutch's blood—seeped onto the sleeping bag, too. Silver turns his palms. Blood is so common here.

White light ends his inquiry with an explosion of sudden pain.

"You're awake," a voice says.

A dizzying blur surges then begins peeling away. The room returns in slow order; the bunkbeds, the cool floor Silver lays on, the pounding in the back of his head. For some reason he can't move his arms. He is on his stomach. An awaiting supply of pain bursts through his shoulders as he struggles to find that his hands are bound together at the wrist. Behind Silver's back, the oppressive strength of zip-ties tighten and slack.

"Where am I?" Silver moans.

"You know where."

Silver's chin swipes the floor as he strains toward the voice. Standing there is Hutch, his back to the closed door. He is in full cammies, rifle in hand; its barrel pointing down at the boots Silver did not hear.

Hogtied but ungagged, Silver can't help but wonder if the terror he now saw reflected what their team's prisoners eyed from their own weighted bellies. No, for whatever dire act required subdual, the look in Hutch's eyes was bereft of all reason. The full bloom of madness does not diminish when Hutch lets his own rifle clatter to the floor. As big as the world, the cracked buttstock, eye-level, reveals to Silver what had knocked him out.

"Well," Silver says, laying his cheek against the floor. "You got me. What now?"

Hutch stands like a statue. "When I knew God wasn't real," he says, speaking in a way that strikes Silver as something rehearsed, "I was sick. I felt like I lost my best friend. But now I know...what? *What*, you ask? Well, I'll tell ya Corporal Josh fuckin' Silver. Jesus don't seem to do much. Gramma prayed an' prayed, we all did, and Gramma's dear old cancer ate her alive. Hell, ol' JC never produced a...a Shantak neither. But *they* did."

The zip-ties suddenly feel tighter. "Hutch, you're telling me—"

"What I'm *tellin' you* is that I know which side to be on."

"So, the range? The way you've been goddamn acting—"

"You don't gotta worry about me anymore, TL." Hutch spits.

"Who have you killed?" Silver asks as a swirl of grim visions pass his eyes.

"Killed?" Hutch smirks. "Ain't killed no one. Not yet."

Silver speaks with slow, meditative agony. "What about the blood, Hutch? On the bed?"

There is a moment where nothing happens, then Hutch begins to unbutton his blouse. Silver can, and at the same time *can't*, believe it. Hutch stands, holding the flaps of his blouse like open wings. "It's a new day," Hutch says, admiring a red, oozing version of the Sect's symbol he'd carved deep into his own chest.

Silver shuts his eyes. Screaming may help. A scream may also be all it takes for Hutch to bend down, pick up his weapon, and carry out the first act for his newfound religion.

"What happens now?" Silver grimaces, afraid of the answer.

"Well, dear old TL. We've been through a lot, you and me. But it's time I acquire me a Humvee. There are people who're gonna be real, real happy to hear *you* killed yerself too."

"Hutch! Dude!" Silver shrieks. He wiggles like a worm. "You don't have to do this!"

And then, at that moment, Silver sees it.

At the door is Mangler, in his gym clothes, eyeing Hutch's rifle that lays black on the floor.

Silver feels Hutch climb over then kneel down beside him. Like most who were withering away in the MEK, Silver had conducted his manhunt with his rifle in hand. Now that rifle is in Hutch's hands, its cold barrel pressing against the flesh under Silver's chin.

Mangler reaches down. He shoulders Hutch's weapon and begins to rise.

"Oh, but I do," Hutch says, pressing the rifle's upper receiver against the floor, getting the angle just right. "Sure gonna be a sad report." There is nothing, no time. "I am sorry, Silver."

The Mangler keeps rising. He looks at the front sight post with both eyes open. Sweat gleams off his face and makes slick his cheek's weld against the buttstock. The safety selector is on, and he now flips it to Fire coolly as Hutch does the same. Mangler aims, fires, and the back of Hutch's head explodes in a spray of blood and brains and hair.

25.

18 2222C SEP 05

"In the end, it is all over," Silver says, not knowing what he means.

Silver and Greene are drinking liquor. They are on top of a HESCO barrier, watching tracers from a losing gun battle far off in the night. Greene puts out his cigarette then lights another.

Mangler is getting a final workout in. No weights, just running the inner-perimeter. Every twenty minutes or so they believe they see him, running, a dark shape amongst the shadows.

Perhaps a mere distraction from the utter crumbling, Silver's mind has grown entranced by the potential meaning of his visions and their culmination into his potent dream. Greene seemed okay with not talking about Ellers, or Nguyen, or now Hutch. Greene seems okay with sharing the biting taste of some more Jack and not talking about death, or the lunacy that had become the parts of Iraq that are out there in front of them. This sad sendoff of Greene's, Silver knows, has become an escapism; obsessed over if Greene's returned books had anything new to say.

"Okay," Greene says. "Dreamlands. Did you enter through what you could call *enchanted woods*?"

"No."

"Were there any man-eating spiders?"

"Nope."

"A town with a bunch of cats runnin' around in it?"

"No."

"There may be no meaning, man."

Silver breathes and says nothing. Hutch's death had been the last straw. Hours ago, he and Mangler were cut orders back to the States for immediate psych evaluation and removed of their weapons.

"This may sound conceited," Silver says, "considering the world is about to end an' all, but I want my goddamn name cleared."

Lieutenant Ashton's ranting and raving was one thing. So was the entire battalion sowed to silence over not one but two deaths, in a single team, coming from its own team members' hands.

The full day and then some had cleaned up Hutch's trailer and forever tarnished the sparse remnants of Stygian 2-3. Mangler, at least, had made himself feel better; nearly bashing a shit-talker's head in against an aluminum wall. Silver, though, he'd suffered the concerned stares, the whispers they thought he didn't hear, from lunch to dinner to crawling up onto these HESCOs to burn useless over a goddamn dream.

"Well," Silver says. "Fuck, I guess there's nothing left to figure out then."

"Maybe. Maybe not. I do have one thing. That page with the symbol, where is it?"

This hits Silver like a round in the chest. He has no idea.

"Yeah," Greene says. "Thought so." He waves the folded page in Silver's face then hands it over. "Hutch stole it too. Found it in one of the books."

Silver mumbles.

"After I did, though, I got to reading."

"Tell me you said some shit out loud. At this point—"

"Nah, man." Greene laughs in a way a friend would when looking at one in no place to laugh themselves. "But I did find something else. Remember what you told me that interpreter told you? Something about there being portals. He wasn't joking. Well, I translated one."

"One what?"

"A portal spell. But it's weird—well, weirder than all the other shit on that page. It's specific. There's a way to close it once it's open. Says when it opens it won't be open long though, and, and this is the real kicker, it says it has to be executed in some other world, not ours."

Silver looks up at the stars. "I wonder if, maybe if I *went* somewhere the other night."

"At this point, dude—"

An artillery weather balloon is falling, falling, falling down upon them. Greene curses as he almost falls off the HESCO. Dropping out of the sky with such suddenness, the malfunctioning balloon nearly forces Silver to scream. Then he slams shut his jaw and steadies himself. Flying in low and hot, the two specks of neon aren't arty Chem-Lights—

—But wild, green, glowing eyes.

If Silver still had his weapon, this monster, this fiend would be shot to death, or undeath, or whatever foulness these things had to fear.

"What are you?" Greene gasps.

"I am...that which is becoming," the fiend says, its green eyes beaming the HESCO.

Silver pulls Greene out of his own rifle sling, aiming the weapon right at this monster's mouth then, without thought, pulls the trigger.

Greene opens his eyes.

The wraith laughs and wrestles with the barrel, having knocked its round up, high, into the sky where now below, those in earshot, if this creature departs unseen, would, too, soon speak of Silver's insanity. Silver senses this—this sudden pull back to him being still in the MEK, still not wanting to empty a roaring mag into: "Friend or foe?" he growls, watching a hand coolly slide off his weapon.

That which had flown in upon them then smirks. "Shooting without positive ID?" it needles, folding lifeless legs onto the HESCO. "Where's your confidence, Marine?"

Silver doesn't, then almost does, then doesn't give Greene back his rifle.

Not that it would have done much good. Greene is entranced, not only staring at a rancid stump where a hand had been, but at all the rotting skin.

Silver crouches. He doesn't look at Greene or this rotting, seated, one-handed oracle; only where the oracle's one hand now buries itself in the dust atop the barrier. Silver looks up.

"You need to hear there's a way to win," the *oracle* says. Its voice is shrill, like the cords are still tearing, devoid of all joy. Winds blow and the stars shine.

"I don't give a shit," Silver says, answered with cackles and tales of crawling out from under brick, flung from a hospital bed, rising like a festering sun.

Greene's eyes say what his mouth is unable.

Silver still holds Greene's rifle.

"I hear their talk on the winds," it says, foam frothing. "You lost some, yeah? Me too." Their visitor is without weapons, having flown in *under the radar*, as it once may have said. With its hand it strangles the air, as if gripped around someone's neck. It says, "Burning all in Hell, they are. But what we still wouldn't do to choke the life out of those who put them there. Am I right, warrior?"

Silver and Greene stare at one another.

"You want revenge?" it says through more foam. "Go to the house, you know the one. Put a bullet in the brain of that little bitch, the one calling the shots."

Silver's heart hears something his brain has yet to. This messenger, this American afflicted with black magic worse than either Hutch or Nguyen; its eyes, its hovering above the sand, its awful words for their dead: *Why is this giving me so much?*

When Silver was nine he'd struck out at the plate, costing his little league team the win. His coach, a fat, rough, mustached drunk; proceeded to ostracize the young short stop. "Boys, just swing better than Silver—whose team you on anyhow, son?" Next game Silver struck out wildly. Over and over. Taking cuts at balls so low and high even his own father howled from the bleachers. His team hated him, his coach looked for just the right moment to backhand him then threaten to send him down to the minors, and, after he'd sated an unnamed desire, he cracked out a grand slam.

At eleven he'd found himself in a canoe with an angry water moccasin. The mad spill into prowling alligators and out onto dry land where another moccasin lunged for his leg was the greatest day of that or any other summer.

Because it was sure defeat! Survived and surmounted by mere luck and two swimming, leaping legs. Because once his coach, his team, the whole world hated him he was free to swing for the fence. This against-all-odds was where he performed his best.

And at fourteen, Silver climbed over a train track fence to fight back two junk yard dogs. A neighboring dunce had been the first one over, satisfying a dare some older punks had given from the lofty height of a tank car. Soon, one dog had seized Silver by a shoe and the other his forearm. The rescued boy scurried over the chain-link and was gone. The others, screaming on top of the train, descended onto the rocks to lob them over at a vulnerable stretch of tugging fur.

Never before had greater fear gripped him. The snarling, the pain beyond description, the competition to pull him apart at his seams. He was going to die. And somehow, from some dark secret place, deep inside, there ringed a lunatic's thrill.

The dogs, long dead, were not why he joined the Marines, but the ordeal had uncovered early why he later would. Not for God or Country. Not to climb the ranks. But to die, gloriously, and in battle.

For a cause not even known to him. It was all ultimately futile, the struggle, but the struggle was heroic.

The fiend's words were giving him back this oddest of strengths.

"You're that dude," Greene says. "That dude from the hospital...Miller?"

Miller nods.

Every teacher, every drill instructor, every Recon legend harder than nails and worth their salt; they had all teased and tormented Silver, out from his sorry shell of self-pity; to be what he always was.

"You got that, warrior?" Miller sneers, rising above them, looking up at the moon. He flies away.

Silver yells into the air. "There's never a—a little bitch at the farmhouse."

"It must be that kid," Greene says, getting back his rifle.

"She'll be there," Miller calls back. "And so will I."

26.

18 2328C SEP 05

5th battalion's armorer wakes up to find the barrel of Greene's rifle pressed against his forehead. Greene is not in the darkness of the trailer. Silver is. So is Mangler. The pair hovering amongst the shadows.

"Mac," Silver whispers, easing the pressure off. "Need to borrow your keys." Wordless and confused beyond comprehension, the armorer looks over at the Mangler.

"Can do it one of two ways," Mangler says, shining a flashlight on the other armorer, also no longer peacefully asleep. Hogtied and gagged, the other armorer nods and energetically *mmhmm*s to his frozen roommate.

"Okay," the Marine named Mac says, unable to see in Silver's smirk or Mangler's menace what's about to happen.

Greene had felt and smelled the hot breath of the messenger. He'd heard the rant, knew the words held a validity that had arrived with infections of the same magic that had turned a zombified Nguyen into a one-man hit squad. But to join Silver on this most insane errand—insane even by new standards of flying people and obedient Shantaks? Call it too much Listerine liquor. Call it too many days spent listening to annihilation over furtive radios. Greene had agreed, but only if Mangler came too.

That was no hard sell. Greene and Silver caught him on the way to the showers.

"Some," Silver had tried. "Some—"

"That sniper that went missin' from Charlie Surgical," Greene said.

Silver explained Mangler right into his gear then relieved Greene of his rifle for a second time.

"Okay," the armorer now says, moving to a wall locker that holds the keys to the battalion's armory.

Silver snatches them. "Count to a hundred then cut your guy loose. I get pinched at the armory, Mangler here is gonna come walking again through that door."

"Y-you—you got it, Corporal. What do I tell them though when… whatever is gonna happen happens?"

"Tell them," Mangler says, "Stygian Two-Three had one last mission."

At Greene's Quadcon waited the man they'd all agreed Silver and Mangler are going to "kidnap."

"'Bout fuckin' time," Greene says, holding a thin stack of 3x5 cards. He looks up at the sky. High, white, and judgmental, the full moon was a run of the mill unit commander. Its light glows down, illumining the duo to their look of utter suspicion. "Get in," he says, ushering them inside, shutting the door and flipping on a light. "Jesus…"

The two look like they'd raided six armories. Back with them now are their pistols, pistol holsters, a wide, hungry drop pouch apiece, hanging low on the hip. In their hands are their primary weapons; Silver's M4 and Mangler's M249 Para SAW; ready for the ammo belts crisscrossed over his chest. In each man's butt pack are the answer to when the radios they didn't bring would've gone down. Foot long, silver cylinders; ready to be popped into action. Purple smoke, red star clusters and a white star parachute; signal flares roll and clank against rigger's tape and packs of QuikClot. Silver's rig sags with loaded magazines. Twenty-nine rounds per, leaving one out, ensuring the lethal health of the mag's crucial spring; a trick an old recondo had taught him in a shoot-house he'd never see again. In their rucks are water and more ammo, compressing spines to a misery their war-painted faces hide under the dark curtains of their helmets.

Mangler finds a seat, mitigating his many burdens to plop down with a comic sigh. Greene stops trying to count the grenades dangling off of him, resting his eyes instead on what is strapped to Mangler's back: a green, 84-millimeter, unguided, single-shot, recoilless, smoothbore, anti-tank monster killer.

"Nice AT Four, Mang'," Greene says, waving his 3x5 cards. "But I think I got somethin' better."

Silver had given Greene back the page, this time with an idea. Now all three put Greene's cards in their pockets. Greene had sounded and spelled out into English a selection of spells. Along with crude drawings of the monsters on the card's backs, the plain white rectangles are the final contribution to the trio's arsenal.

"Hell," Mangler says. "We don't need you at all now."

"Shit," Greene says. "These are the easy ones."

Silver says to Greene, "You got that weird portal one? Who knows what we'll need."

"Yep," slapping his cards, "everything you can imagine, and then some."

"Oh, I almost forgot," Silver makes a whirling motion, reaching for something pinned to his ruck. "You'll need this too." He tosses Greene back his M16A2, equipped now with a twenty-nine-round mag of its own.

"All right," Greene says, sighing, slinging a weapon he's never fired in anger, or in fear. "But I ain't puttin' on Cammie paint."

The guard tower had loomed in the distance. In the dead quiet of a wartime camp, the crunch of gravel echoed under their boots, against aluminum walls of trailers and the low concrete offices where

Marines and sailors slept. This night was black as the rest, lit orange by odd lights in areas where generals had deemed worthy.

The three had marched calmly up to the main gate, standing under the guard tower in wait of whatever MP was going to climb down and greet them. Small foot patrols left the MEK every once in a while. They could pass as no exception. Recon guys kitted to the gills and a crypto-linguist attachment, no suspicion necessary and a sure go ahead if only—

"Shit," Silver whispers, turning away from the sergeant.

"Corporal Silver?" she says. She'd descended the tower with her rifle slung behind her back and radio in hand. The lights bolted to the nearest T-barrier have made the mouth of the MEK black-orange-black-orange. Scowling, she steps through the striped shadow. "Looks like you got op status back."

"Yeah," Silver says. "Just the other day."

"I noticed they took your name off the roster." She surveys his teammates. "Congrats."

Mangler smiles.

Greene fails miserably at not looking off-put.

The MP squints at Greene's face, then casts a doubtful eye back to Silver.

Reading her, Silver says, "Black dudes don't need to Cammie up, not as much."

"I knew that," she fires. "I went to Marine Combat Training. I take it you guys want me to open the gate."

"If you don't mind. We'll be back in the morning."

The list of charges is impressive. They'd *kidnapped* Greene, pulled a gun on one armorer, falsely imprisoned another, and stolen enough weapons to lay siege to Leavenworth. Odd then, and Silver sure took note, that her acceptance of this lie relieved him so greatly. He hopes she doesn't notice the humungous sigh he lets out as she turns and radios up to the tower.

Greene pats Mangler on the shoulder.

"Say again," she says. "You're coming in weak and unreadable." The voice on the other end isn't coming from the tower, but someplace else, deep in the martial bowels of the MEK. The hair on Silver's neck stands up. "Say again."

The crackle of the radio fizzles and a clear voice then reports: *"APB, two recon marines held another marine at gunpoint and pillaged an armory—"*

The voice dies as she drops her radio, eyes wild and white like a deer. "Stop right there!"

"Whoaaa," Mangler soothes, affirming his grip on her rifle.

Silver grabs her by the back of her head, cupping his other hand over her mouth as she belts out a muffled scream. "*Shhh—* goddamn it!"

Silver and Mangler peel her down to the gravel.

"We aren't gonna hurt you," Silver says, still negotiating her teeth.

Footsteps hurry down the tower.

"Shit," another MP emerges and says. This baby-face has his own rifle, shouldered, and he comes through the shadows trying in vain to stop its barrel from shaking, pointing it at Mangler, Greene, then at Silver's head.

"Shoot him, shoot him!" the sergeant screams.

Silver hadn't realized he'd let go of her mouth. A barrel trains a bullet right at Silver's left eye.

Then a hard crack rings in everyone's ears, except the young MP's. Silver's would-be killer drops to his knees then hits the ground with a *thwump.*

"Man," Greene says, holding his rifle like a baseball bat. "Hogtie that bitch and let's go."

"So much for the kidnap alibi," Manger says as they finish.

The two guards are dragged into the darkness under the tower; one squirming and cursing into rigger's tape, the other out cold with a bandage wrapped around his battered head.

Silver had gone up in the tower. Now his cohorts hear him running back down. Mangler and Greene know something is wrong.

"They changed the damn code," Silver spits.

"We ask homegirl here," Greene says, picking up his rifle, "she's just gonna scream again."

"Yeah," Mangler says, getting his ruck back on. "And homeboy isn't about to answer shit."

Silver looks at Greene. "Plan B?"

###

"This should've been Plan A!" Mangler says, gazing up at the beating wings.

"Probably a good thing they see this," Silver grunts, slipping once, twice.

The slime-coated scales make for no easy mount. Silver tells Greene to make the Shantak lay flat on its belly. Greene says the word, lowering the Shantak's horse head below the barriers. Both MPs now scream into taped muzzles.

"Heee's awake," says Greene.

Taking the space of a 5-ton truck, the back of the gravel-clawing night-breather rubs against their legs.

"I can't believe we're doin' this shit," Greene says, holding up his palm to see a snotty string of slime.

"You guys ever see *NeverEnding Story?*" Mangler says.

Greene, who is sitting middle, turns to shake his head at Mangler's excitement—not that he's saying *no*—he's seen the movie.

Silver, up front, seats his rifle across his thighs. By all earthly comparison, it is like straddling a humungous alligator; the hardness of the scales, the restrained reptilian power ready to burst at a moment's provocation. He looks over his shoulder. It would have shocked him if he'd known he'd looked at his last team with eyes brighter than a smile.

Greene and Mangler sit like rollercoasterers wearing helmets.

"I don't know how many points of no return we've crossed, Alex," Silver says to Mangler. He doesn't ask them if they are ready, just that Greene say the word.

Fleshy spikes line the beast's back. Each man grabs hold, switching; behind—forward, as Greene sends them up, up into flight, flapping idly for an instant, then tearing forth into the night air.

27.

18 2352C SEP 05

Silver winks back at the nearest, blinking star. By Greene's word, they follow the black ribbon of the MSR, flying across the moon as tears freeze to their faces.

They are riding the wind, incapable of not yelling to one another; a boyish dream come true. A boyish reprieve from the height they could fall from or the biting cold not a one had prepared for. There's MSR Mobile, and how dismal the vacant Michigan looks. Powerlines are soon below then behind them. From this height, Silver sees their next collecting feature. The Shantak firms its wings into a glide, bringing them above then southward to the contorted knot of an intersection.

The team sees everything, the black, deadly land, the curving hardball incased by roads on either side. Like the prior movements, Silver has Greene keep them *on* the most southern of these three, a helicopter's view above the route until gaining altitude and veering hard. Now they follow the dirt road, pushing deeper south as berms appear, waving and rippling as they speed past.

"Ready for this, TL?!" Mangler screams over Greene's shoulder.

Silver grips a horny spike with both hands. Turning he says, "Fuck no! Greene, start taking us down!"

Greene yells in Arabic. Both ends of Mangler's AT4 catch the wind, seesawing up and down in whichever way their Shantak moves them low under the night.

I wish they were here, Silver thinks, shivering. *Both of them.* Silver would give almost anything to have Hutch and Nguyen hugging cold spikes of their own. In strange, foul ways the enemy that awaited had not only taken their lives but mutilated their legacies. Sure, Hutch and Nguyen's fates were not the same. But, as Silver purses his lips and wipes sand from an eye, the team-ripping frustrations, in fact, rip away. Even if Hutch didn't, Nguyen deserved the chance to make things right. And despite Hutch's sad, ignoble end, as the pockmarks of potholes begin gaping below, the certainty of what had to be facing them makes Silver want to give even Hutch a shot at redemption.

"I've been lookin' for those damn green lights," Greene yells.

"Me too," Mangler yells back. "Haven't seen shit."

Silver had been as well. Eyes cast dutifully south, battling sharp sand and sharper cold, he had yet to be given a clue in the night beyond the magic they'd summoned.

Timed well, the Shantak lowers them onto the canal road right as its bulk begins to fade.

For several seconds, Silver crouches, thinking or fretting in the exact spot where the Shantak had become thin air. The moon and midnight stars hang above. Among them they could fly on another.

As the seconds stack to a minute, the words of an old operator ring in Silver's head like a bell. It was the way of recon. For all the uppity cheer about jumping out of planes or finning to an objective underwater, the safest, most efficient, most effective way, is, and always will be, as the old Master Gunz had said: *"To walk the fuck in, then walk the fuck out."*

A few more seconds of whispering over whether flying too close will or won't tip off who or what is in the house, they set out on foot. The silence of night is bad for covert affairs; but Silver is more concerned with the openness of the canal road. This is a road Humvees had trekked, a bare stretch left omitted from foot patrols. Too easy to get caught out with no cover or place to run. With the Nahr Abu Ghurayb rushing by, Mangler and Silver grab Greene and dissolve. In the shadow of the nearest berm, Mangler and Silver don

NVGs—gear Greene didn't bring. Greene grunts, hardly audible over the rush and gurgle.

A long moment passes before Silver holds out a thumb.

Mangler responds.

Greene doesn't. He looks around, confusedly, only reaching some remote semblance of calm when Mangler squeezes their effectively blind teammate on the shoulder.

Silver waves his hand forward, taking them by way of careful feet and the military crest of the berm to the flimsy, creaking bridge.

"You think *this* shit's gonna hold us?" Greene whispers. He grabs onto the back of Silver's ruck. Greene's eyes are adjusting but he is still unable to see the loose rock that almost sends him sprawling.

"Mangler," Silver whispers without taking his eye off the bridge. "You're heaviest." The bridge, as all else out here, seems…affected. The wood seems warped, the wobble Silver's exploratory step causes is severe, too severe, as if the planks had been aged unnaturally.

"It feels okay," Mangler replies, having pushed past and firmly planted a foot.

Get it together! Silver thinks.

Following the black bulk of Mangler's ruck and sideways AT4, they run beyond the canal's southern road, making their way down the berm and back onto solid ground.

Silver's hair had stood over the danger of open areas, but his cortisol surges as he looks through monocular weirdness at familiar objects now mutilated. A leaky tractor; shot to junk and upended. Trees—charred skeletons, their palms now brittle hands, breaking in the wind. Silver cannot help but think of his dream; as if his mind had unwillingly wandered to a place now pushing, prodding, making its way outside the veil.

As they head south-southwest, they form a file. Silver is out in front. Mangler takes up their vital six.

Greene, surviving the middle, still can't really see.

As rooftops began to appear Silver begins to cuss. He had tried to do so furtively, though no dogs are around to make an alarming bark. He gives the signal.

"What's up?" Greene whispers. "Why'd we stop?"

"NVGs just went down."

"Mine too," Mangler says, unsurprised.

Cast off behind the row of houses and down the road sits the farmhouse. A speck under midnight, their objective awaits. The home looms, and the powers holding its bricks down to their very foundation now radiates far.

Silver waves them forward. "Let's move."

28.

19 0048C SEP 05

"Get down!" Silver yells and hits the dust.

Greene flails and fights with his sling as Mangler disappears behind the black trunk of a palm, shouldering his SAW.

From the same group of houses as before, gunfire has erupted.

This time, however, above the bright flashes flies a formation. Silver counts three, screaming back to Greene as Greene stares wide-eyed at the approaching Nightgaunts. Mangler belts out his first burst, putting out the flame of one AK as two others emerge.

When Silver's rifle jams the hollow click shakes Greene out of his terror and down into his pocket. The crypto-linguist pulls out his cards, flipping through them in a flurry, realizing right then a deep flaw in his plan.

"I can't see shit!"

"Flashlight!" Silver cries as the formation bears down on them, emptying half a mag into the lead monstrosity of the winged V.

But batteries are all dead, Greene learns, hurling his SureFire and thanking God he smokes. The wavering flame of his Bic soon illuminates the words, the beasts, and the name he now reads.

One appears, then another. Then another. Hunched, vaguely human, new things shamble to the forefront. The Nightgaunts swoop in, spreading their talons. Greene's monsters hop forward then leap into the air, latching onto their foes with enormous claws. The weight and fury of these skirmishes comes crashing down, impacting all around them like mortars as Greene calls forth one more friend.

Greene points a finger at the houses. He sees the new thing, how it turns with his direction, how its eyes burn yellow as the muzzle fire it now hops toward.

"What the hell are those things?!" Silver slaps in a fresh mag.

"Dimensional Shamblers," Greene says, breathing so furious his breath looks like tusks. "They probably won't be here long, we—"

"Mangler!"

"Yo!"

"Bound! Greene, you follow me."

"Rog'!" Greene yells over the shrieking still rolling in the dirt.

Mangler is set. "On you, TL!"

As Marines had done for a century, they attack as two elements. They leapfrog, Silver and Greene running to a patch where they drop to a knee and fire their rifles. Mangler responds in kind, fanning out, running past their position to lay suppression fire as they rise once more to lay siege to the nearest house.

The row is a goddamn Christmas tree. Every window, every doorway, every inch of the parapets and from behind every hard corner wreaks steady fire. Only insanity would prompt the Marines to charge forward so recklessly. But they, just like the world, have gone insane.

When Greene's Shambler hops through a doorway, the chaos of battle unfogs just long enough for them to hear the screams. In the absence of return fire, Silver and Greene make it all the way to the protection of a bongo truck. Now laying cover fire, Silver and Greene both hear and feel Mangler as he blasts his way to their side.

"There's gotta be a million of 'em!" Mangler yells.

Indeed, the Sect had grown, and the watching farmhouse was a landmark of great import. How many fighters shot they could not know, but their position had seemingly one cure.

Greene never let go of his Shambler card. As he'd ran, he'd gripped it so tight he'd turned it into a sweat-marred ball. He uncrumples it now and delivers a small horde into the nest of houses. He had tried to measure which spells would offer the best chance against the disfiguring evils that had sucked on that sniper so horridly. For his best guess he had been right. Shamblers hop after men, out into the night, disappearing with their screaming prey; clutched by a pair of fangs.

"Holy shit!" Mangler shouts. "Greene got one."

The vomiting of the houses made for easy cleanup. Greene takes his eyes out of his sights, looking over them at a silhouette that no longer moves.

The monsters seem to blip, in and out, of the house, their view, the world itself; returning with long arms to carry on their errand. Mangler smacks Greene on his helmet so hard he almost topples over. "Looks like we got a monster those chickenshits don't!"

Silver picks off those the Shamblers are still chasing. Mangler tosses a grenade. And Greene, suffering a glee undreamed of, puts down another through the long barrel of his M16. And then, soon, like the Shamblers, the enemy is gone.

There is no way for them to know what happened to the Nightgaunts. All that remains are the flings of still-settling dust and the vicious tears dug shallow but severe into the face of the earth.

"What we do now?" Greene asks.

"That." Silver points to the farmhouse.

29.

19 0106C SEP 05

"*This* is the farmhouse?" Greene says it. "It's—"

"Not what you expected," Silver says.

"No, man. Not really. Not like I wanna see a demon or anything, but all that radio traffic...there's not even a bullet hole."

To Silver, as to Mangler—busy clipping in a new SAW drum as they walk forward— the *boredom* of the farmhouse strikes them very much the same as it does their tiptoeing crypto-linguist. And that is what unnerves Silver the most.

Their first encounter; the place was shot to tatters. The second; repairing itself with a magic they'd come to confront and be so affected by. Why the source of such evil was sitting silent, Silver could only guess, knowing a few steps more that guessing would no longer be needed.

The front door is unlocked. Greene is asked to watch the roof. Silver and Mangler stack up and execute a two-man clear, entering the space where Nguyen died. Greene soon follows, alerted by the same sounds that are drawing the warriors into an open room.

Unbeknownst to the three, they have entered the same room where Sergeant Paul Miller had once watched a farmer get devoured, and in it now stand two members of the Sect of the Faceless God. The Iraqis are armed, adorned in black and behind rigs weighed down by ammo. But they are waiting, curiously. Their AKs, though shouldered for battle, point at the room's barren floor. Never had Silver stared so hard, so hateful. The rare glimpse of an enemy who moved and fought with potshots and IEDs. He may have stared until a killing urge overtook him, if it weren't for what stood between them.

Guarded is the child, and beyond her, along the wall, crackles the outlines of a circle. Though its hollow green leaves visible the brick inside it, Greene knows they are witnessing the spasms of an eager portal. Its lining comes alive. The child removes her kufi, exposing the side of her head ripe with rot.

"Man," Silver hears Greene mutter, "Where the fuck's that sniper?"

Mangler has his SAW shouldered. He awaits something from Silver, but Silver—like him—can only listen as the child says, "Welcome."

Silver doesn't raise his rifle. He taps his trigger with the tip of his finger, bouncing his eyes back and forward; from her guard's hands to her growing sneer.

"What are you?" Greene says.

"I am nothing. As are you."

From the corner of his eye, Silver watches Greene dig into his pocket; thanking something other than God when Greene doesn't pull out a card.

"I…" she continues, "am the great power that brings forth the greater. Dying planets circling the horn of Taurus. I have seen the stars of Abbith. Death, forever, is the great sower of seeds you know not. But you shall."

She rips open her blouse. Where prepubescent breasts may have been, hideous, long, grey tentacles unfurl; reaching out to wrap around the necks of her guards.

Both are lifted off their feet, gagging and kicking. One drops his weapon, ripping into the smooth flesh with every finger before wrapping his legs around what chokes him.

Greene says nothing. For the first time in his life, Mangler stands stupefied; not shooting, not moving, not breathing as the Iraqi's legs let go and the room rings with the sick crack of neck bone.

Whatever Silver's thinking is lost as all three duck. The final guard, more robust than his strangled contemporary, lights the room alive. The sheer noise of an AK-47, in a room, spraying wildly against brick and corpus alike—Silver returns fire, as does Mangler, as does Greene, all prone, blind, pressing under the weight of the melee.

The second neck breaks. The body of the man slams against the floor, staring Silver in the eye, still flopping as Greene and Mangler scramble to their feet.

Silver rises too, unable to take his eyes off the holes they put in the last Iraqi. All three check themselves, sharing in their disbelief: none of them are hit. They pat their thighs, stomachs, the rigs on their chests. It is called operating in the black—a state where one's senses depart, brought on by a lack of preparation. But they had prepared... as best able for a mission which took them under winged Nightgaunts into a room swelling with gun smoke. Nothing exists. Not the dark, nor the room, nor their hands still searching for their own blood.

"Oh, shit." Greene says, pulling Silver back. "Look."

She lays on her side, coughing up the deep red of an ordinary girl. Someone's round had found her. Lit in the green crackles, she laughs. "With my end—comes the beginning. You will pain and you will rot, the Faceless—"

Silver raises his M4 and finishes her, putting a round in her head as she giggles her way to a second death.

The green circle instantly dims, then it is gone.

Silver listens. Greene is rummaging in his pocket. Then the room is lit in the natural, healthy orange of a Bic lighter.

"You know," Silver says, looking at the lifeless tentacles, too pelted by madness not to be optimistic. "We bring her back there's no way they can dismiss us."

Mangler uses his boot to roll over a strangled guard. "He'll have that tattoo, too. What you thinkin'?"

"I'm thinking," Silver says, "we ride Shantaks all the way back to the MEK, right down into that goddamn motor pool. With these three in tow."

All goes dark.

"Shit." Greene strikes the lighter back into action. "Yeah, but if she's dead, the magic might be dead soon, too."

"Then we better be quick," Silver declares.

As Greene whips out the Shantak card, Mangler and Silver look at one another: the survivors. Their stares become grins, then smiles, then outright, uncontrolled hilarity.

"Come on," Silver says, rubbing his hands. "Let's drag these fuckers outside."

Light reappears.

Silver turns to see the circle, back on the wall. *"Greene!"*

The circle is different now; its interior glowing brighter and brighter and brighter—a light that is not green, but rather the hue of a swimming sunset.

Greene drops his lighter. "Oh my god."

The child's words: death had opened the portal. And through this, they see a man—a shape, tall, slender, black as shadows at the bottom of the world, standing silent in his darkened robes.

In his shock Silver reverts back to a memory. He was in a squad bay with a bunch of other brand-new Marines. They'd pulled up folding chairs, all in the hopes of watching through a portable DVD player the movie *The Ring*. As that girl crawled through the TV, so too Silver thinks, does the leg of—

"Nyarlathotep," Greene stammers, saying it again, raising his rifle: "It's fuckin' Nyarlathotep!"

The Marines take aim, but the Faceless God—the Crawling Chaos—raises but a hand. None can move, which they confirm through a spree of pitiful squeaks and calls to one another. Their enemy, the enemy of all, stands tall and still. There is a face attached to the top of this pillar of shadow, one which does not smile nor sneer. He only looks.

"Sorry I'm late!" a voice yells.

The horror waves his hand, the same that had suspended the Marines. The portal behind him pushes and grows, becoming all the walls around them. His look of growing curiosity, scanning the frozen three from boot to human skull sends them screaming.

"Sorry, I'm late," the voice says again. "But this magic's a bitch!"

Miller, Silver realizes.

A rotting, tattered version of the man flies in; dripping, stinking, and careening like a headlong torrent, right into their enemy.

30.

UNK

Out of the small, smoke-choked room went the Marines, up through velvety voids of starry blackness. Time burst, galaxies swirled and crashed, suns swelled and suns withered, and Silver still flew through the voids.

Then by the sluggish way of forever the universe and what lay beyond its outermost quasars cooled, and what had been there was there no longer. The cosmos, its assorted clutter of rock and ice and go-nowhere light; all choked in a final death of heat spreading thin, wisping off unseen matter into the freezing nothingness of eternal obliteration.

And then there was light again.

A solar wind, cut off a newborn star, toppled and warmed the flying Marine. There were stars and planets and volcanic moons; dead and alive. One such orb he descended upon, scaled and shingled with tiny, eternal rows of military trailers. From mountain peaks hidden by rusted cloud, Shantaks called their homing cries.

Celestial rocks became comets, and comets exploded into salvos of blue, white, and cadaverous grey, and Silver still glided through an atmosphere, red and yellow. Cries cut through the scape as Greene and Mangler and that demented thing flew and fell near. The Shantaks, high above, cry and call from their rocky perch when the four Marines land softly on the dirt.

"Where are we?" Mangler says, brushing himself off.

Silver stands. About them, the Iraqi houses; the ones they'd been shot at from, the ones prior they'd raided—they all still stood. The small dirt road leading away still led away, in its benign straightened path, shooting south over the horizon. But this was not their world.

"I think I know," Silver says. The horizon is laden with rust, wispy; an eternal sunset bathed in rancor. No two trees looked the same. Their palms, their blackened trunks; all hiding from the eye.

"Miller?" Greene says, "You're Sergeant Miller, right?" At his feet lays the breathing corpse who'd sent them all spiraling here. "You saved our asses, man." Greene kneels down to lift him.

From the mutilations, from the burning eyes, burned lips and knotted limbs, Miller whispers, "Just let me be."

"Holy Mother of God," Mangler says, spinning around.

"We are in like some parallel dimension," Greene says.

Never in Silver's dream did he see what he sees now. From the triangulation of the homes, the trees, the road; the farmhouse should have been what he looked upon. And, in a sense, he did. The farmhouse, its shape, its height, its squatty existence was all there, but the white and yellow of the Iraqi plaster and its windows had all been replaced by the balefulness of hard basalt, glittering black in the haze that crawled over them.

Long past fear, longer past the filmy bubble of what *is* that had cloaked his brain being skewered, Silver observes their surroundings. More than one moon scowls down from the pinkish sky, perhaps together giving the basalt farmhouse its freakish glimmer. Beyond the house, their beams shine down onto rolling hills. One summit is malformed and nearer the Marines than all the rest. Alone, disconnected by some alien geology, the hill's white top burns like bone under the haunted light. The water Greene offers Miller gets spit up. Mangler can only gaze at the black walls of mirror-polished basalt as Silver squints his eyes over at the hill.

The farmhouse has a door.

###

"Yo, what the hell you doin'?" Greene watches as Mangler shoulders his SAW and then places his hand onto the shining knob. He stops. Greene is still kneeling beside Miller, having given up on water but not yet on the ghastly man's struggling attempts to rise. "If somethin's in there," Greene calls, "it can stay in."

"Door's locked."

Greene doesn't hear Mangler. Miller's coughs and gurgles are too loud. Greene says, "We gotta get out of here." His words are meant more for Miller than the daring Mangler who doesn't lie twisted and supine as Miller does. For whatever effort the once sniper had hoped to inflict, he had flown in weaponless, pale as pearls, smelling danger close to his unwelcome tomb.

Then it hits Greene like lightning.

"Silver," he says, fast, panning the horizon. "Did *he* come through that...that wormhole with us?"

And Silver's face says everything.

The lone summit with the white top, it had been no hill. For where the dull lump had rested under the alien sky, there is now a gargantuan mass, rolling and slugging and slithering itself toward them. Too massive to fit in the house—too massive to fit in the house if the black walls had warped and ballooned so its unyielding knob had been the size of Silver's helmet, this true terror towered above, high, shifting and weaponizing its amorphous pallor.

"Alex!" Silver cries.

Mangler sprints to his brother's side, now seeing the nightmare. Rolling their way like a wobbling tank, the thing displays tentacles, fingers, claws.

"That's him!" Greene cries, gasping over their shoulders, his eyes as wide as the ones sprouting out from the changing flesh.

The eyes scan wildly—then burst.

"Silver," Mangler says, understood entirely. Silver forces his eyes from what approaches, unable to unhear the squishy flaps and farts as it covers more ground. Silver frees the AT4 from Mangler's ruck, placing it in Mangler's hands.

Mangler spreads his legs, extending and flipping the arming components, sighting in on a fanged head of eyeless, earless hulk. Silver rips Greene out from behind the weapon's back blast zone. Both Marines aim their useless rifles as the mass gets closer, and closer, and closer as Miller suddenly flies into the air.

A flame thunders out the back of the AT4 and is gone. A violent speck zips low above the ground.

"You got 'im!" Greene cries.

The explosion had rattled the rocks at their feet. And the monster now writhes, its skin blackening and bubbling, appendages all gripping the great hole ripped wide in its stomach. The injured abomination tries repairing itself, growing ghastlier with the slaps and gurgle of its ever-changing form. That face, swollen clear of human dimension, appears then rips itself in two. Arms sprout, and then they coil, unable to catch with its talons the vile chunks that spatter all over the Marines. Its death throes inhale stones out from the earth that a wrecker couldn't budge and then crushes them to powder. Sergeant Miller, flying above the carnage, pukes and curses as he avoids whips by a tentacle or the swatting of a colossal black hand.

The thing is not dying.

Silver and Greene fire. Their rounds plop into the corpus, opening holes that spew the vilest of fluid. Mangler drops the AT4, reaching for his SAW still dangling on its sling.

Greene and Silver both look when Mangler curses. One of the stones the monster had lifted had not been obliterated but shot like a reciprocal missile, missing by inches the man, but reducing Mangler's SAW to a disabled hunk of hanging metal.

The Mangler arms himself with a grenade as blisters resembling another hand, striped and colored by a reptilian green, grips another stone and hurls it. This stone is as large as the warrior it screams toward, and this one doesn't miss.

"Oh my god," Greene says, breathless, motionless, pulled out of his paralysis by a violent tug from Silver.

Facing the end, Silver and Greene, sent by unthinking impulses, run for the cover of the farmhouse.

Up above, Miller avoids a high flung rock, slipping past the monster's newest tentacle, joining the crying, frantic two as a live grenade remains clutched in Mangler's lifeless hand.

"He's dead," Greene cries. "Mangler's dead." The growl of their foe is behind them, but it won't be for long. The god rolls and he amasses.

"Guys," Miller whispers, in abject pain, somehow sounding clearer than any noise allowed against the thunderous din. "Guys, I…" His eyes, which had glowed in this wickedness that had assaulted their world, roll back then they pop forward in the most violent blaze. His screech stops Silver from reloading his M4, and together Silver and Greene watch as the madman, finally consumed, soars skyward, chanting. "Absolutely nothing, as you, as you."

"Our rifles can't do shit," Silver says, holding back tears. Then he screams and turns to tug at the door. Silver plops down. It would be but a moment more. "What can we do?" he says, hopelessness washing over him.

Tentacles wrap around the corner of the basalt wall, dripping slop as they pull their owner closer. Silver sees Greene's eyes, how they spark with fear…then of something else. Greene drops his rifle and begins digging through his pockets with both hands.

He looks up at Silver. "The portal spell."

Silver stutters.

"It's this or nothin', man." Greene holds up a card.

"I'll hold him off." Silver rises to his feet, running out from the shadow of the wall, out into the red alien dirt and begins firing.

Greene curses, tossing the card and digging back for the correct one. He hears Silver change magazines more than once before he, trembling and with no time left, holds the card and begins to read.

He is dazed. Blood runs from his nose, into his mouth which he spits to the ground. He realizes he had just been pummeled. He picks up the portal card then he sees a horrific thing. Miller floats above him, clenching his hand like talons. Opening, closing, he moves his rotting fingers, kneading the air.

"We stay," Miller says. Deeper than the rasps of that girl, it washes over. "We stay in this hell together."

Greene goes for his rifle. In an instant, punches and teeth and curses not in English nor Arabic engulf Greene as he's slammed again to the ground. The slow hollow echoes of Silver's rifle continue to ring. Through the ensuing flurry, Greene can see the rust of the clouds wetting into a sanguine bruise. Greene grabs Miller's wrist, punching into that fetid mouth with a closed fist until Miller has no choice but to fly away. When Miller does, a long black tentacle reaches far and fast, seizing him in its coil.

The hideous form flings fluid and claws at Silver. The Faceless God flexes and reshapes, hurling Miller himself into the course of Silver's fire, ceasing for but a moment the Marine's sting and sending the other howling wildly into the air.

###

Greene scrambles to his feet, brushing away the dirt from the ground in which he fought until he fingers again the card ready in his hand. He reads.

A short distance away, Silver is down to grenades when it happens. There is a whine and a great flittering. Light, white and clean, bounces off the basalt house's foremost wall. The whine grows into a great bang, and the portal opens.

"Silver!" Greene cries. "Miller! Let's go!" Swirling, floats the lightning laced window back to their world.

Spinning on his heel, Silver sees the miraculous blandness of the Iraqi berms. His M4 done, his pistol empty, he runs headlong, past Greene, diving through the portal, rising instantly to his feet.

"I got you, dude!" Silver yells with his back to the Iraqi night, pointing his weapon by instinct into the swirling silver mirror as Greene climbs.

Greene screams. Blood sprays Silver's face as the cruel end of a claw exposes itself.

"No!" Silver screams, seeing the terrible wound, reaching in and pulling Greene through.

Greene falls onto his back. Light from the portal shows the extent of his wound, punched through his back and continuing through the chest, allowing him only the faintest gasp from ruined lungs.

Silver holds Greene's hand, repeating the battlefield *You're doin' good, you're doin' good* as Greene stretches a finger and slowly points. The portal has not closed. And through it, the Faceless God stares.

Greene still grips the card. With great effort he speaks.

On the other side, that fatal claw now chases Miller like a fly, catching him by a leg and sending him down, thumping against the alien earth so hard bones crack and brake. As the portal shuts Silver watches: the monster is pulling Miller, closer with each constriction toward a great cavernous mouth.

Silver holds Greene's hand and bites his own. Miller, flailing and howling, is getting dragged right by the crushed body of Mangler.

Miller calls out, "Yes, yes, take me!"

Miller drives his entire force into his arms, using them like feet to crawl. There is the whine again, whistling in Silver's ear as he peers through the opening, now no bigger than a fist. Miller grabs onto Mangler's helmet, wrapping his fingers around the chinstrap until Mangler is dragging behind.

Silver vomits—the thought of his teammate going into the gnashing maw that tugs Miller ever closer.

Miller makes a sudden pull, letting go of the chinstrap and prying the grenade out of Mangler's hand. With his teeth he pulls the pin, spitting it out, laughing, yelling his allegiance to the utmost evil. It explodes right as he's pulled into the mouth.

The portal closes.

Greene lies dead in the field, but if he were alive he'd sigh and say myths, now not, spoke of how nothing could kill the great Nyarlathotep.

But Miller's death was at least final. A better way to go than what waited, perhaps.

31.

01 2101C OCT 05

Nights later, after he was told his combat-meritorious promotion was ripped up and thrown in a burn pit, Silver lays on his cot, cast in shadows under a fizzling lightbulb in the MEK's makeshift jail. Charges are still being consolidated and rewritten. He went UA. He'd forced Greene, assaulted armorers and depleted his battalion's armory of an arsenal that—no matter how hard military investigators had grilled him—they've thus far been unable to recover. And no one believes him why. Speculation is still growing, rallying that he, soon to be Private Joshua Silver, was and has been all along an agent of a now-quiet, deplorable sect.

He doesn't sit up as Captain Ashton addresses him from the free side of the cage. "That must've been some hike," Ashton says. "Fireman's carrying Sergeant Greene all the way back from that farmhouse."

Silver slips a wry laugh; the platoon commander's silver bars on his collar are so new and shiny. Silver rolls onto his back and stares up at the lightbulb. He could try once more and explain they'd never find the body of Corporal Alexis Mangler, that the still-going search was even more futile than the one they'd spent on Nguyen—another person rumors were solidifying he'd done wrong. He could try to explain that Greene had wanted to go, that would maybe spare him one year from the millions awaiting him in Leavenworth.

"Silver," Captain Ashton says, apparently still stuck on how the wound that killed Greene was beyond the scope of any bullet. "What killed him? A little honestly won't hurt at this point."

Silver turns his head but nothing else. "That paper you guys now have."

"That paper you guys have, *sir*."

In a moment of fury, Silver had used Greene's lighter to burn all the cards. Now, like many things, he wished he hadn't. "Have someone who reads Arabic read it out loud."

"You know," Captain Ashton finds a stool and sits down. "Those MPs at the front gate you'd mentioned, they aren't exactly talking— well, that sergeant isn't, but that PFC you busted up," Ashton laughs, "he's sticking to his guns. An *enormous bat-dragon-thing*, it appeared out of nowhere and three motivated devil dogs *jumped on it like a horse*. Yeah, I figured you'd perk up for that. Crazy, huh? The side effects of being bludgeoned in the head? He'll be gettin' his med board soon enough. Hell, you two might be on the same flight home."

"I've already told you how Sergeant Greene died, *sir*. Oh, by the way, congrats on the promotion."

Captain Ashton's face goes red. He snarls, standing up and kicking away his stool. "Look at you. You were a goddamn recon team leader. Now what? You have about as much power as the Iraqi that sweeps this floor."

The talk is over. Silver listens to a series of doors slam as the officer walks out into the night.

###

In a nearby office, clean and proper, an investigator warmly greets his fellow captain. "Captain Ashton," the investigator says, taking his legs off a desk littered with papers. "Happy you are here. I've been talking with our new friend here and it gives me great pleasure that this small gesture is one step towards healing so many wounds, so recently caused."

The investigator nods to a corner of the room, alerting Captain Ashton to their guest. Standing, straightening his thobe, a local holy man meets him with a handshake. *"As-salamu alaykum,"* the Iraqi says.

"Alaikum salaam," Captain Ashton remembers to say, smiling and bowing, cutting an impressive figure. The imam is old, but not grey. "Do people ever tell you how great you look?"

"Oh," the imam switches effortlessly to English. "All the dates, mister. Good for the health." His eyes twinkle, he bows so low the captains get giddy. The holy man rises, stroking his beard. "Your brother, he explains you have something for me?"

"Indeed," Captain Ashton chirps, taken out of the warm bath of adulation. "Captain Klein," he says, prompting the other captain to hold up proudly two bags of evidence. "I believe these are yours."

The imam's eyes widen. Despite his oddly dark attire, for its somberness the charming Iraqi seems ready to float on a cloud. "Ah, yes," he joys. "A most gracious thank you."

In a clear evidence bag is the ancient page Silver had found, the one Greene had translated. In the other rests an old book by H.P. Lovecraft, taken by a sniper the coalition forces no longer hope to find.

"We are sorry for any inconvenience we have caused you," the investigator says.

"Yes," Captain Ashton affirms, taking the imam's hand and shaking it profusely. "And know that we know Islam is a religion of peace."

"Indeed," the old Iraqi says. "Indeed, brothers. And know I shall call from the minarets your deeds. My followers, they are many."

At last, the imam is escorted from the office, out to the front gate where an official escort of Humvees awaits him. Before he goes, he and the captains walk and talk as friends bent on sharing their peace with the world. Past the makeshift jail they'd walked, for reasons unknown to the Americans a point in the route that made the imam stop and seem to sniff the air. He utters under his breath words only he understands; its tone convincing Captain Ashton they'd somehow offended him. After a barrage of apologies they send him off, belted into a fine up-armor Humvee.

Silver sits up in his cot. Maybe it is due to having trekked in a magic world, or maybe being touched by Nguyen, or being lathered by pieces of a faceless god's most hideous guise. Whichever, Silver sits up in his cot, a smile growing across his face. His eyes flash a determined green.

END

ABOUT THE AUTHOR

David Rose is a former Recon Marine and veteran of the Iraq War whose poetry collection *From Sand and Time* won the Robert A. Gannon Award for its depiction of Marine Corps life.

An active member of the Horror Writers Association, Rose's fiction includes *Amden Bog* and *The Scrolls of Sin*. He lives in Orlando, Florida.